The UNEXPECTED FIND

Toby Ibbotson

Scholastic Children's Books
An imprint of Scholastic Ltd
Euston House, 24 Eversholt Street, London, NW1 1DB, UK
Registered office: Westfield Road, Southam, Warwickshire, CV47 0RA
SCHOLASTIC and associated logos are trademarks and/or
registered trademarks of Scholastic Inc.

First published in the UK by Scholastic Ltd, 2019

Text copyright © Toby Ibbotson, 2019

The right of Toby Ibbotson to be identified
as the author of this work has been asserted.

ISBN 978 1407 18624 5

Printed by CPI Group (UK) Ltd, Croydon, CR0 4YY
Papers used by Scholastic Children's Books are made
from wood grown in sustainable forests.

1 3 5 7 9 10 8 6 4 2

www.scholastic.co.uk

For Mika

THE STORM

When the hurricane finally came, it came quite suddenly to the town where William lived. A few gusts of wind pushed leaves around on the pavements, and some big drops of rain pitter-pattered on the roofs of parked cars and bus shelters. But then there was a stillness. It was so still that it seemed odd – as though the wind was taking a great big deep breath.

And then…

It began.

WiLLiAM

The storm roared through the town like a crazed elephant, or a pack of mad wolves, or an invisible giant with a huge vacuum cleaner. Slates were ripped from roofs. Things flew away: washing, wheelie bins, bikes, garden furniture. Sheds were flipped on to their backs, doors were ripped off their hinges. It was exciting. But it was frightening too. People get hurt in storms like this.

As night fell, William lay in bed listening to the storm. There were a lot of different noises: from the street came the rattling and flapping of anything not nailed down, and the howling of the wind as it screeched round corners and whistled through every narrow opening or archway and played mad music on gutters and drainpipes and chimneypots, each one a different note. There were indoor noises as well, as objects that never normally moved, moved. Window frames creaked and complained. The hatch in the ceiling that led up to the loft lifted an inch and fell back with a *thump*, giving William a start each time. The fireplace in his bedroom that had been plastered over years ago suddenly groaned as though some sorrowing prisoner was walled up in there.

It was almost impossible to sleep, and William wasn't good at sleeping at the best of times. Outside his window the wind wailed to be let in so that it could run howling through the house. In fury it rattled the windows and lashed the glass with rain.

Quite close to where William lived was a park. It was called Canal Park after the old industrial canal that ran along one side of it, and here the storm did what storms do: it raged, putting every living thing to the test.

Here I come, it roared. *Now, let's see what you are made of.*

Who has dug their roots deep, and worked a thousand slim fingers into the clay?

3

Who can hold on and who will let go?

Who is old and dry and tired?

Who is supple enough to bend and bend and bend some more, and who will bend only so far before they break?

There are only two ways to survive such a storm: be immensely strong, or be immensely weak. In the centre of the park, where a great ash stood, the almighty wind blew one final enormous blast and celebrated its greatest triumph before passing on, racing away to the northeast.

Only a single eye saw the great ash fall.

When silence fell at last, William got out of bed, went to the window and stood gazing out into the grey morning light. It was a strange light; the sun was coming up, lighting the overcast sky from underneath as it did. There were no shadows. It was like stage lighting – everything perfectly clear and not quite real.

He hurried into his clothes, and sneaked downstairs and out of the house. It was so early that he saw just one other person – a tall figure wearing a wide-brimmed hat, walking with long strides in the opposite direction. As William passed on the other side of the street, the person raised his hat and called, "A very good morning to you." Apart from that, only the faint sound of a car engine somewhere disturbed the stillness. The storm had washed the air clean, and swept the streets bare; leaves, rubbish and branches had swirled into piles in corners and against walls. A flowery tablecloth hung from a power line like droopy bunting after a giant party, thought William. It could have flown across the Irish Sea from Galway Bay. It could have come from Jamaica or Guadeloupe. Some poor lady was probably wandering about looking for it under the hibiscus bushes or among the pineapple plants. William tried to remember what pineapple plants looked like. Did they grow on the ground like cabbages? He wasn't sure.

He came to the pair of stone pillars that marked the entrance to Canal Park, and walked in. There was plenty of amazing destruction to look at – not just trees. Waste bins had been rolled along for hundreds of metres and come to a standstill in odd places, and one of the lamp posts that lined the canal towpath was bent almost in half. The canal itself was full of floating debris that should have been somewhere else: branches and crates – even a park bench was bobbing upside down in the water. But it was the storm's final victim that William wanted to visit, and he walked straight to it, right to the middle of the park.

The huge old ash had been the tallest tree there. Now it lay stretched on the grass: its vast crown looking like an entire forest, its trunk as long as two railway carriages and its enormous roots naked and pointing at the sky like monstrous fingers. There were leaves and twigs everywhere.

William walked towards it, fascinated, and looked down into the crater that had been left when the roots were ripped from the earth. He saw grey clay, stones, sand, bits of root sticking up and, at the very bottom of the hole, something else – something smoother and darker in colour. William clambered into the hole and crouched down, getting very dirty in the process. He started to scrape away the hard-packed clay.

It was an hour or so later that William walked

back along the towpath. Putting his hand into the pocket of his anorak, he closed it around the thing he had found under the roots of the ash tree. There was still a lot of clay clinging to it, but by the weight of it he thought it must be made of metal, and he was sure of one thing: that ash tree must have been hundreds of years old, and anything lying right under its roots must be even older still. Of all the things in William's collection, this was one of the most interesting.

JUDY

If the storm was an elephant on land, it was another beast entirely on water. Inside the boat on which Judy lived, the wind had racketed around the boat and made it wrench and tug at its moorings like a nervous horse. The draught in the little stove had sometimes been so fierce that it threatened to drag glowing coals right up the chimney, only to spit them back a second later and spew enough smoke into the room to make Judy cough.

It was a pretty thing, the narrowboat. Painted green, with windows and hatchways picked out in the brightest yellow. Pots of herbs in the well-deck – rosemary, basil, mint – and, in pride of place, a bay tree sat in a large wooden half-barrel. There was even room for a small folding garden chair. It all looked very homely. Once the boat would have housed a whole family, with children playing on the roof, washing strung on a line, and a bargeman puffing on a pipe in the stern as he navigated the locks and waterways of industrial England. But now only Judy and her dad lived here. Well, normally.

Judy finished putting things to rights on deck and stepped back inside through the narrow stern door, and down the short ladder into their living space. To her left was the little cooker, the sink and the fitted cupboards that made up the kitchen – except it was called the galley, because of being on a boat. Next came the living room, with a decent-sized table and a bench fixed on one wall and covered in cushions. On the other side were bookshelves and a cupboard, and between them stood an old iron stove, a proper one lined with firebricks that would burn wood or coal. Further down came the bunk beds, and opposite them the very small bathroom and a door that led out on to the well-deck at the front. Judy turned on the light, lit the gas stove and put on some water for tea, reminding herself to start the generator later and let it run for a few hours to charge the batteries.

Judy made her tea and frowned. She had a little job to do, but she didn't really want to do it. Still, she took a digestive biscuit from the cupboard above the sink and reached up to a shelf to take down some paper and a pen before sitting at the table. She thought for a moment, and, after a while, she started to write:

Dear Mrs Knowles,

I am sorry to say that I am away on business next Thursday, and will be unable to attend the parents' meeting. But I trust you will keep me informed of Judy's progress at school. She speaks highly of you, by the way!

Yours,

Reza Azad

Judy studied the result. Despite herself, she was pleased with it. The trick was not to think too much – just let the writing flow from your hand. And she was really good at Dad's signature now – and so she should be, she had practised it for a whole afternoon and written it out about a thousand times. But she thought the best bit was the last sentence. Mrs Knowles was only human; she wouldn't pay attention to anything except the bit saying that Judy liked her.

"Judy, you are a genius," she said to herself.

Judy sat back and stared out of the little window nestled into the opposite wall. She missed her dad, badly. He would have loved that storm if he had been here. She remembered the evening when she'd come home from school to see him sitting by the stove. He'd tried to act like he was fine, but she wasn't having any of that. She had seen straight away that something was up. Her dad told her that he'd received a letter from his dearest friend, Rashid.

"*So?*" she'd asked. Why was a letter such a bad thing?

"*Rashid is making his way to Europe, and he seems to have made it to Sweden. The letter was posted from there.*"

"*Sweden? Then he's safe?*"

"*I hope so. But something doesn't seem right. He*"

should have called me by now. Rashid is not just any refugee, Judy – you know this. His work, his knowledge..."

Judy never knew how to react when her dad started talking like this. It all sounded pretty unbelievable, but her father was no liar, she knew that much for sure. She watched as he spoke about Rashid probably travelling under a false name, perhaps being followed. She knew where the conversation was going. So when her dad finally said the actual words, it didn't come as a surprise.

"I shall go to Stockholm, and talk to some people. I have a friend or two at the university there. I shall find Rashid..."

Dad had given her a questioning look.

"Can I leave you on your own for a little while? Rashid is my oldest friend. I owe him more than I can say. If it were anyone else..."

"It's all right, Dad, I'll be fine."

She had been on her own for a long time now. At the beginning she had enjoyed being completely independent for the first time in her life – going to bed when she liked, doing her own shopping and cooking, that kind of thing. Her father was the best person in the world, but sometimes he did still treat her like a child. So she had been glad of the chance to show him that he didn't have to worry about her so very much all the time. And she had known it wouldn't last for ever, so it was a sort-of holiday, really – a break from being told what to do.

But it wasn't a holiday any more. It had gone on too long. He had said a few weeks and it had turned into three months and eight days. She tried not to get in a state about it, tried not to imagine all sorts of bad stuff that might have gone wrong, but it wasn't easy. The waiting, the not being able to tell anybody anything, the not having anybody to ask for help... It was too much for her and Judy didn't really know what to do.

STEFAN

After the storm fled from England, it swept out over the grey-green North Sea – wind against tide, wave crashing into wave – so that there was nowhere for the water to go but up, in geyser-spouts of spume that were whipped away as clouds of salt-laden spindrift. When the storm had had its fun, it threw itself across Kattegat at the coast of Scandinavia, and roared northwards to find some real forest to play with.

Stefan Petterson was walking back from the river when the wind started. He'd had no luck fishing, and he'd lost one of his best lures. Stefan could hear that the wind was already freshening into a gale. It roared like a distant waterfall in the pine-

14

tops far above his head. But down here the air was still, among the boulders covered with grey and yellow lichens, the bilberry plants and ferns that spread across the forest floor, the tiny spruce and pine, slowly building their strength for the time when their huge guardians would finally fall and they too would have their day. All was calm. A squirrel scrabbled up the arrow-straight red-brown trunk of a ninety-foot pine, stopped for a look, and scuttled out of sight. But when Stefan came up on to the road and into the open fields he felt the wind properly, and saw the birches thrashing their heads about to shake out the last of the autumn leaves. It was getting dark, and the heavy clouds above him were almost purple. *No snow tonight*, he thought. But soon. The whole countryside was waiting. A week or so ago two cranes had flown in wide circles high above the farm, calling. They had been joined by others. Then they formed a v-shaped skein, and were gone, crying their farewells.

By the time Stefan had got home, dumped his gear in the shed, gone into the kitchen to steal a bun and gone back out to fill the wood basket and chop some kindling, the wind was blowing really hard. In the stand of pines behind the house, every tree was bent in a great arc along its whole length as though some mythical hero of old was stringing his bow for a wild hunt in the sky. The tarpaulin that covered the stack of next year's wood was gone. He found it under a lilac bush and had an interesting time trying to get it back over the woodpile and tie it down while it flapped and struggled and generally misbehaved. He got cold. There was a chill in the rushing air that said winter was waiting in the wings. At last he could take the wood-basket, kick off his boots in the porch and go back into the kitchen. His grandmother was at the stove.

"There'll be some people losing their pensions tonight, Stefan. All winter playing pick-up sticks, and a shameless price for storm-felled timber when you do get it out."

"Hmm," said Stefan. He had just nicked another cinnamon bun, still warm from the oven, and was biting into it.

1

The following morning William walked along the towpath on his way to school. About a hundred years ago the canal had been like a main road, and all the things that were made in the town's mills and factories had been taken down to the coast in barges pulled by horses. But now the big barges were gone, and so were the horses. First had come better roads, and then lorries. And then the mills and factories had closed one after another. Nobody made anything in the town and the canal was soon full of rubbish and dead rats and a horrible smell. But then things improved. The council had had a big clean-up and had made Canal Park, which was long and not very wide but was a lovely place to stroll and feed the ducks. Now there were narrowboats moored along the towpath, many of them very well-cared-for and painted in cheerful colours.

William couldn't resist taking his find out of his pocket again and having another look. He stopped on the path, and was studying its rather odd shape so intensely that he didn't notice the two boys coming towards him until it was too late.

"Hey, it's Weird William! What've you got there?" said one of the boys. He was the bigger and fatter of the two and his name was Tyler. William didn't like being called Weird William, but a lot of the boys in the class above him at school called him that, so he wasn't particularly surprised.

"Nothing really," said William, and put his find back into his pocket.

"Nothing? It didn't look like nothing to me," said the other boy, whose name was Josh and was smaller and thinner than Tyler and about twice as clever, which wasn't a very hard thing to be.

Josh whispered something about William's pocket to Tyler, who said nothing for a moment, before a light went on in his brain and he gave a screech of laughter.

"I said it's not anything," said William, and tried to walk on past them. It was a mistake.

"No, you don't. We just want a look. I bet it's something you've nicked. Maybe you're not Weird William, maybe you're Worthless William," said Josh. Tyler thought this was pretty funny too. Josh grabbed hold of William's arm and tried to wrench it loose from the pocket, but William held on with all his might, even as Josh shook him about like a rag. Then he lost his balance and fell. He kept a vice-like grip on his find, and because he couldn't use his hand to break his fall, it was a hard one that just about knocked the breath out of him.

After that things became confused.

Josh was bending over him, still trying to shake his arm loose, when William heard a shout. He squinted up and saw a small stone bounce off Josh's forehead. Then, in sort-of slow-motion, he saw the skin part and watched Josh's expression change from a stupid grin to shock. Josh let him go, and slapped his hand to the place where the stone had struck. Red blood started to ooze between his fingers and run down the back of his hand.

"Aargh!" said Josh, and sat down with a *thump* on the towpath.

By now William was curled up in a ball, and he had his eyes tight shut. But he heard Tyler's voice.

"Josh, are you OK? What did he do?"

Josh just whined and then William heard footsteps and a different voice, which spoke from right above him, saying "Are you all right?"

"I think so," he said, and he opened his eyes in time to see the lower half of a pair of legs in jeans and trainers step over him and stand between him and the boys.

"Well, that's lucky for you two," said the voice.

"It was you, was it? You're gonna get it." Tyler stood up from where he had been kneeling beside the injured Josh and advanced towards the new arrival, clenching his fists and looking murderous.

Now William sat up and paid attention. It was too interesting not to. He saw that the new arrival was a girl, with long, dark hair and a very determined look on her face. He watched as she moved off right to the edge of the towpath. She didn't seem to care about Tyler at all, just turned her back on him and walked away, saying over her shoulder,

"Run off home to mummy, you useless lump."

That really got Tyler going. He yelled at her and charged like a rhinoceros, and William wanted to close his eyes again but he didn't, and he was glad he didn't because Tyler thundered up at full speed and at the last second the girl sort of twisted round, stuck out her foot and pushed all at the same time. It really was very neat and quick, and Tyler seemed to propel himself, almost without any help at all, over the edge of the towpath and into the canal. He was pretty big and heavy, and so was the splash. William looked at Josh. He was still moaning and crying with his hands on his forehead, and you could see that he was just making a fuss. The blood was already dry and caked on his fingers. He wanted to make it seem worse than it was. William had seen people do that before, but they were usually small children. Tyler was invisible below the canal bank, but William could hear him shouting and splashing about.

The girl had walked back and was standing next to William. He looked up at her.

"Will he drown?" he asked.

"Not a chance. It's only waist deep. Muddy bottom though, and the nearest steps are a hundred yards away. He won't get out in a hurry."

She paused. "Can you get up? We should be off before that other twerp decides he's not actually dying."

William stood up and looked at her more carefully. She was wearing a grey woollen jumper that was about ten sizes too big and almost came down to her knees and she was breathing quite hard. He could tell by her eyes, which were a nice dark brown colour, and the way her mouth was sort of thinned out at the edges, that she was not only angry but also worried, almost a bit scared. He couldn't understand why someone like her should be scared. She had just polished off Josh and Tyler with no bother at all.

"Are you OK to walk?" she said.

William got to his feet. His shoulder and left knee were a bit sore, but otherwise there was nothing much wrong with him.

The girl reached out a hand and brushed off his sleeve. William flinched a bit, but he let her do it. Then she asked, "Why did they start on you?"

William remembered. His hand flew to his pocket, and felt the hard shape there.

"They wanted … something."

The girl's sharp eyes had followed his hand to his pocket. She shrugged.

"They would have used any excuse," she said.

And because she really didn't seem to care whether he told her or not, William told her.

"I found something interesting under the fallen tree. I don't know what it is. But it's special, I'm sure." He took a deep breath. "I can show you if you want."

The girl looked at him very seriously, as though she knew he had said something difficult.

"Thank you, but I wouldn't show it to anybody if I were you," she said after a moment. "That'll make it less special."

They set off along the towpath. Tyler was still spluttering and yelling, and Josh was trying to pull him up the side of the canal. They walked on in silence for a while.

"My name is William Parkinson."

"I'm Judy."

She walked fast, almost angrily, and William almost had to trot to keep up with her.

"I got into a temper, and I shouldn't have," she said quietly.

"But if you hadn't, then I wouldn't have my interesting find any more."

She stopped abruptly, and turned towards him.

"You're not the kind of person who looks ahead very much, are you?"

"Yes I am, or I'd be bumping into things all the time."

She laughed, which made William feel a lot better.

"Exactly what I meant. You don't even know what I'm talking about."

"What *are* you talking about then?"

"When people lose their temper, it has consequences. Cause and effect. Karma. Whatever. I don't need that right now."

Judy stopped on the pathway, lost in thought. *It's like she's not really here*, William thought. But then her eyes snapped back into focus.

"Look, William, you can get to school from here, can't you? Those two will have gone the other way."

So William walked on towards school by himself. It had been a very interesting morning already.

In maths, William sat quite far back, with lots of desks and pupils in front of him. Next to him sat Mr Gordon the assistant. Mr Gordon was quite a nice person, and William didn't mind being assisted. But today William had noticed that Mr Gordon seemed a bit tired. It was Monday and Mr Gordon was often a bit tired on Mondays. Once he had actually nodded off, which was a very good description, because his head had suddenly dropped forward and then bounced back again as though it was on a spring. He had looked at William and said, "Sorry about that, I had a night on the tiles," so William had wondered if he'd been climbing roofs. Mr Gordon had said, "No, not exactly, but you aren't far off," and they had gone back to the maths book, with Mr Gordon pointing at stuff, and William looking at it.

On this Monday Mr Gordon managed to stay awake, but there was quite a lot happening in the classroom, as usual. The two girls in front of him were giggling about something, and a boy kept asking Mrs Dench silly questions, and she was trying to keep her temper. But William didn't really have time for school, and certainly not for maths. He always had more important things to do, like writing in his notebook, and now that he had cleaned up the thing he had found under the fallen tree, he very much wanted to look at it some more and work out what it was. Then the classroom door opened, and Miss Jameson who sat in the office put her head round the door.

"Excuse me," she said, "but Mr Greaves would like to see William Parkinson."

William didn't mind; he liked Mr Greaves the headmaster. He knew about almost everything, and he had told William about Roman glass and said that there were certainly Romans around here a long time ago, and that he would look out a book for William to borrow. Another time William had been examining a fire extinguisher and it had gone off and sprayed white powder all over the corridor, and Mr Greaves had gathered everybody in the assembly hall and said, "Who is responsible?" and William had said, "It was me." Then Mr Greaves had said, "I hope you all heard that. That is what is known as a straight answer to a straight question, and there are plenty of people in this room who should take a leaf from William Parkinson's book." William had been worried about that, because he didn't want anybody to take leaves out of his book, but nobody actually had. William and Mr Greaves had cleaned up the mess in the corridor together, and they had talked a lot. He had told William that taking a leaf out of someone's book was a metaphor, and meant following someone's example.

William walked down that same corridor now and went straight in to Mr Greaves' room. There were already quite a lot of people there, sitting on chairs arranged in a ring. Josh and Tyler were there, and so was Judy. Josh had a huge plaster on his forehead. Next to Tyler was a lady with very blonde hair all piled up on her head and very red lipstick, wearing shoes with very high pointy heels. Next to

Josh was another lady, who had a tracksuit on. She was wearing shoes that William thought must have hurt her feet a lot. They were so small, and the rest of her was so big.

"Come in, William," said Mr Greaves. "These ladies are Josh and Tyler's mothers. I talked to your mother, but she let me know that she's not very well and so couldn't come in."

William took a seat next to Mr Greaves. Judy was sitting opposite him, but he didn't say anything to her because he could immediately see that she was completely closed and didn't want to talk to anybody. Her dark eyes were directed straight at him, but she wasn't looking at him at all. Mr Greaves looked at Judy and said,

"And of course your father really should be here, Judy. We can leave this whole matter until he can get away."

"No," said Judy. "It's fine, I don't mind."

"Well, you *are* old enough to make that decision. But we may have to talk to him later."

"Yeah, I know."

Mr Greaves gave a slight pause and cleared his

throat.

"Right then," he said. "We have a situation here that we need to discuss."

William looked up at Mr Greaves. He had a long nose with a sort of dent at the top, almost a little shelf that was just right for holding his glasses in place and stopping them from sliding down to the tip and falling off. On the top of his head was some thin brown hair, and on his brow were quite a lot of wrinkles. Once when William was in class two he had asked Mr Greaves why he had so many, and he had answered, "The question is, rather, why there aren't more, William."

Mr Greaves continued. "William, could you tell us all what happened in Canal Park this morning?"

William was silent. He thought about the fallen tree, and the great big hole it had left in the ground, and now … now he would have to tell Josh and Tyler and the mothers everything. He tried to open his mouth, but it wouldn't open.

"You were walking to school along the towpath, weren't you?" said Mr Greaves in a kind voice. "What happened then?"

"*Oh then,*" said William, "Then…" And he started to talk. He had only got to the bit where he had fallen down when Josh started in.

"He's lying, he's making it all up. He's daft in the head, everybody knows that."

Josh's mother put a chubby arm round her son's shoulder. "There, there, pet," she said. "We know you're upset, what with your injury and everything."

Mr Greaves spoke. He never spoke loudly, and now his voice was very quiet and very clear. The staff at the school called it his scary voice. Looking at him, William saw that he had taken off his spectacles.

"Josh, if you call William daft again, I shall exclude you from school for a week and my report on the matter will go to the Local Education Authority."

Josh's mother looked shocked. She tried to talk but Mr Greaves held up his hand to silence her.

"Your contribution will be welcome later, Mrs Bilker. Go on please, William."

So William did. He told them everything. And when he was finished, Mr Greaves gave Josh and

Tyler time to talk.

"We never did anything," said Tyler. "We were just mucking about. Joking a bit. Then she went and chucked a stone right at Josh. It could 'ave killed him, or put out an eye or something."

Tyler pointed his finger at Judy. She didn't even look at him.

"But William was on the ground," said Mr Greaves. "How is that just joking?" Tyler's mother pursed her red lips, pressed her legs even tighter together and sucked in air, expanding her pink cashmere sweater.

"He just fell," said Josh.

"Surely you must take into account that the boy may be … fantasizing," Tyler's mother squawked. "I mean, he's obviously a bit … imaginative, if you see what I mean."

"I certainly *do* see what you mean," said Mr Greaves, in his quietest voice yet, "and so, I assure you, does William, who is neither deaf nor stupid. And who never lies," he added.

William saw Mrs Louch's sweater deflate, and heard air hissing out from between her squashed-up lips. After that William stopped listening. There was a picture hanging on the wall of Mr Greaves' room that hadn't been there last time. It was of mountains, and there were some sheep and a shepherd in the foreground, and a bit of a lake. William thought that it might be a picture from a story, and he tried to think what story it would be.

Then he heard Mr Greaves say, "You can go now, William, thank you," and he saw that everybody was getting up to leave. "I shall inform you all of my decision before the weekend," Mr Greaves went on. "Judy, stay behind, please."

When everybody else had gone, Mr Greaves got up from his chair and stood looking out of the window. He spoke without turning around.

"This is pretty serious, you know. Throwing stones is aggressive behaviour. I could see that it wasn't much of an injury and I know Josh well enough, but he wasn't completely wrong. You could have blinded him."

Judy was still in her chair, leaning forward with her hands stuffed under her thighs, staring at the floor. She muttered something.

"I didn't hear you," said Mr Greaves as he turned back from the window and returned to his desk.

"Very unlikely," said Judy a little louder. She was still staring at the floor. "Velocity, mass, trajectory. His head was at an angle, so one eye wasn't visible at all… The other one had the potential area of impact reduced by at least fifty per cent. And I'm a good shot. I would say my chances of damaging his eye permanently were less than nought point nought three … under three percent," she added helpfully.

Mr Greaves sighed. Jock Henderson the maths teacher had warned him about this. Only last week over tea in the staffroom he had said, "She needs more challenge, you know. She's bored to death."

"I'm afraid people don't calculate probabilities in this kind of situation. They are satisfied with, *Did she throw a stone or not?*"

"Well, I did," said Judy, but more quietly this time.

"Yes, you did. Look, Judy, I really do need to talk to your father – is there no way I can get in touch with him?"

"He's on a field trip. There's no reception up there."

33

"So you say. I can't decide anything until he has been informed. Please let me know as soon as he's back."

When Judy had gone, Mr Greaves sat down at his desk.

"Here comes another wrinkle," he said to himself, and he reached for the telephone.

2

Time passed, and it was Halloween. In the early dark of autumn a bright half-moon shone in the sky, spreading its light across the city rooftops. All across Europe millions of candles flickered on millions of graves, asking the dead to leave the living in peace. William didn't go out on Halloween. He didn't have anywhere in particular to go, and he knew what the street he lived on would be like that evening, with even more people than usual. Christmas and New Year and Saturday evenings after a home game were the worst times, but Halloween was pretty bad too. William lived with his mum on a street called Sydenham Street. It wasn't a very nice street, and at night under the orange glow of the streetlamps it was a bit frightening. After the pubs closed at the weekend there was always a lot of shouting and sometimes there were fights. He had got used to hearing police sirens wailing, or the sound of glass breaking. On Friday and Saturday evenings the thudding beat of dance music from the club across the road went on until two or three in the morning. He was used to that too.

William and his mum had the top flat in a house that had been built for one family but now housed two. You went in through the front door and then straight up the stairs to a door made out of white-painted plywood that had been put in to close off the landing on the upper floor.

The flat was cramped, and almost every room was small: the kitchen at the back was small, and so was the bathroom, and so was William's room, which had room for his bed and a cupboard and a small table and chair. It was a tall thin room with a high ceiling, but he had a window that looked out on to the backyard, and he liked that better than looking out into the street.

William heard his mother moving about in the

bathroom, and then he heard her call,

"William, are you in?"

He came out of his room and found his mother standing at the open door. She had her party clothes on and had done her make-up.

"I'm going out for a bit. Jerry's taking me to a Halloween do up in Brinkside, just for a drink and a bit of dancing."

"OK."

"Aren't you going to meet some friends, or something?"

"No, I don't want to."

"Suit yourself. You can watch some telly in my room if you like. I won't be too long."

"OK."

William didn't often go into his mum's room, even though it was the only non-small room in the house. He thought he might like it better if she didn't smoke quite a lot; sometimes when she brought home a friend and a few bottles from the pub they both smoked, and it really made him cough.

The doorbell rang.

"That's Jerry. Bye." And she was gone. He heard a man's voice say something, and his mother's voice replying, "Don't be daft, he's fine on his own."

William went back to his room and took a cardboard box from under the table. This was where he kept his collection of interesting things. He took out the thing he had found in Canal Park, and sat down on his bed to look at it, as he had done a hundred times since he found it, and wondered what it could be. He had gone back to the park a few days after finding it; and the great tree had already been sawn up into huge logs by the parks department. That meant that he could see the tree rings clearly, and he tried counting them but it wasn't as easy as you might think; sometimes you couldn't see where one stopped and the next one began. But he had got to more than a hundred and twenty before he gave up. So this thing that he held in his hand – this thing that looked a bit like a rusty spoon, or a fork, or some kind of tool – was at least a hundred and twenty years old and it could be even older. It might be Roman, thought William. He would have to ask Mr Greaves if the Romans had spoons and forks. Anyway, it was long and thin, and one end was flattened out and rounded, and the other end was bent over, and the bent over bit was divided into two parts. It might be a spoon if the round end had been flattened under a heavy stone, and it might be a fork if the other end had got bent somehow. But it also might be a sort of scraper. In fact, it might be just about anything.

The person he really wanted to talk to about it was Judy. She was clever, and she was kind too, although she pretended not to be. But he had tried waiting for her after school several times and she always seemed to be hurrying off the other way.

Realizing that he was very tired, William lay down on the coverlet and fell asleep.

On the other side of town, glowing Jack-o-lanterns grinned foolishly from the windows along the street as Judy walked home from the supermarket with a bag of shopping. She had already met two gangs of children dressed up as ghouls and witches and vampires, going from door to door screeching, "Trick or treat!" and greedily grasping handfuls of sweets when the doors were opened. She thought the whole business pretty pathetic and she wasn't in the mood for it. One of her classmates was having a Halloween party, but she wasn't going. Actually, she hadn't even been invited, but that was because nobody invited her anywhere any more. They weren't being unkind, they had just given up trying to make friends with her. And she wasn't being unkind, either, she just couldn't risk making friends right now. Friends meant visits to each other's houses, and sleepovers, and parents contacting each other to make arrangements. It wasn't surprising that she got such good marks at school; there was nothing else to do except go home, do her homework, read for a bit and go to bed – and hope that maybe tomorrow she would find out that the waiting was over. Judy bit her lip. The stories she made up about her father, the forged notes and all that, they wouldn't hold up for ever. Mr Greaves had given her a couple of very searching looks after that stupid business with William. Sooner or later it would come out that she was underage and living alone, and she knew what would come after that.

She quickened her pace.

A side street led off to the right about fifty metres ahead of her, and from it emerged three figures. They stopped under a street light on the corner: a fat one, a thin one and a much taller one.

It only took Judy five seconds to see who they were. Tyler and Josh, and presumably Josh's big brother.

"Oh no, not again," she said out loud. The idea of kicking them in places where it hurt a lot was very attractive, but this time there would be no toughing it out. Judy *had* to stay out of trouble. She stopped, turned round, and started to walk back the way she had come, keeping a steady pace so as not to draw attention to herself. It didn't work. She heard a hallooing behind her and a shout of, "Hey, that's her, that Judy, c'mon, after her!"

Judy dropped her carrier bag and started to run. She wasn't too worried. Tyler wouldn't last more than a hundred yards, and Josh was no Olympic champion either. Big Brother wouldn't bother coming after her on his own. Besides, she could run very fast. It should be easy enough to throw them off. She hared across the road and down a side street, and then left into a smaller street with one row of small terraced houses and a high brick wall. It was a dead end. Judy sighed and turned around. It looked as though she was going to have her chance to do some serious kicking after all. She heard them coming and clenched her fists.

"Down there, she went down there!" Tyler's squeaky shout was unmistakeable. Judy waited, looking back up the row of houses that were faintly lit by a single street lamp. Then she saw that the door of the house nearest to her was ajar. As the two boys came puffing and panting round the corner Judy took two quick steps, pushed open the door and slipped through into a dark hallway.

Ahead of her was a flight of stairs, and a passage that obviously led to the kitchen at the back of the house. A back door would be perfect. She walked fast along the passage, planning what to say if someone was in there. The moonlit kitchen was empty. A half-glassed door led out into a small back garden. It was locked. Back along the hallway. She could hear her pursuers talking just outside the front door. They seemed to be having an argument.

"She went in here, I'm sure of it."

"Is this her house then?"

"No, she lives on a boat or something, she's just sneaked in to somebody else's place."

Josh's big brother Glen was getting fed up.

"I'm off. I can't spend all night chasing girls… Well, not this kind of chasing," he sniggered.

"But, Glen…"

"What? You scared of her then? Too tough for you, is she? And he sauntered off.

Tyler shuffled his feet. "Josh, we can't go in and look for her. I mean, what if there are people in there? We'll get arrested."

All Judy could do now was stay put and hope that Tyler and Josh would give up and go away. She looked back into the depths of the house and saw a door leading off the hall. Judy turned the handle and peeked in. The room was dimly lit. Light came from a thick candle that burned in a tall candlestick in the corner of the room and she could make out an old leather-covered sofa, and a fireplace with an old-fashioned marble mantelpiece. In the grate a gas fire hissed quietly, casting a faint glow on the carpet and on the lower part of a large armchair that was drawn up close to it. The big candle flickered, and shadows danced on the walls and ceiling. Judy's gaze followed the shadows round the room, and she saw a long oblong box of some kind, lying on a low table below the window. As her eyes adjusted to the poor light, she realized with surprise what she was looking at.

Outside the house Josh and Tyler were getting tired of waiting.

Tyler said, "She's not coming out, Josh. I bet she's got out the back way. Let's pack it in, I'm cold."

"We'll just have a look through the window, see if we can see her." They sneaked up to the house, and peered over the window sill.

"J-J-Josh!" came Tyler's screechy whisper. "That's a coffin! And there's a body in it!" There was indeed a corpse in there. The hands, old and gnarled, were folded across its chest. They looked down at a pale face with sunken cheeks, surrounded by long grey hair that was combed smoothly out over the shoulders. The eyes were closed. Suddenly, without warning, the left eye opened and stared directly at

Josh. It was pale blue, with a black pupil. Josh went rigid with shock, and opened his mouth to yell, but no sound came.

Judy wasn't easily scared. She couldn't have lived alone all this time if she was the nervous sort. But when a voice spoke from within the open coffin, her heart missed a beat or two.

"Well, obviously there will be no more rest for me this evening. But at least those little brats have skedaddled."

It was a smooth, soft voice, deep as an organ's base note. You might expect a panther or a bear to speak like that, if it ever spoke. Whoever it was, the voice had a very calming effect on Judy, and she watched in silence as a strange figure sat up, and started to climb out of the coffin.

"Let's have a better look at each other."

The figure walked over to the mantelpiece and switched on two bracket lamps that hung on either side of it. The room brightened and became just a cosy sitting-room and Judy saw a tall figure wearing a loose dark red dressing gown over an ankle-length nightdress and tartan slippers, with shoulder-length grey hair and long-fingered, big-knuckled hands. But what really got Judy's attention was the top of the head, which was completely bald and shiny and glinted in the candlelight, the grey hair falling like a curtain around it. At first Judy thought that she was looking at a rather tall and broad-shouldered lady – a former shot-putter or something. But how often do you meet old ladies with a smooth hairless head like a monk's tonsure? The face that now turned towards her with a broad smile that creased it into a thousand wrinkles had only one eye. Where the other should have been was a crumpled scar.

They looked at each other. The single piercing blue eye gazed at Judy with a bushy eyebrow raised. It made her feel a bit uncomfortable, but she wasn't afraid. Perhaps it was the tartan slippers, or the nail varnish, or the cool smooth voice that said, "Please sit down." Whatever it was, she wasn't scared. So she walked round the sofa and flopped down on to it.

The person turned to the armchair by the fire.

"Alcibiades, remove yourself," he said to a large grey cat that had apparently slept through the whole business. It sat up and licked a paw, then, in no hurry at all, jumped on to the floor and sauntered out of the room with its tail in the air, pretending that it had been going that way anyway.

"Dignity, dignity, what on earth is it good for?" sighed the person as he settled himself in the armchair. "Now then," he went on, "I am known as Andrew Balderson, although at times I do prefer Anthea. It means blossom, you know." He patted the top of his head. "The children of this area, for obvious reasons, call me Old Baldy. And who are you?"

As he asked the question, he leaned forward and Judy felt the single blue eye see right into her from under its bushy eyebrow. Until now she had been quite enjoying herself. It had turned into such an odd night; until now she had never met anyone who slept in a coffin. But the question came so straight at her. It wasn't just a polite query about her name. It made her want to hide somewhere. She felt vulnerable. Something about this person made her feel as if she was losing her footing on a slippery surface.

"I'm Judy Azad. I'm very sorry I came into your house and …" She glanced at the coffin "…

disturbed you. But you saved me from Josh and Tyler, so thanks very much for that. I must go now, though. I have to go home, you see."

Judy started to get up but something in that single eye made her sit down again on the sofa. She sighed.

"I was trespassing, I know. So I suppose you're going to ring the police."

"The police!" Andrew Balderson laughed.

The laugh calmed Judy down again. She still felt off balance, but less bothered about it. It wasn't a mean laugh, or a sneering one, and it certainly wasn't an evil cackle. It was a happy chuckle, the kind that makes you smile even if you hadn't been going to.

"But the door was ajar! I practically invited you in. I think it's you who should ring the police, and tell them you've been kidnapped. The telephone's in the hall, and the number's on the wall. Ask to speak to Sergeant Barnes, and say you've been kidnapped by Old Baldy and he should get down here fast before the tea gets cold."

"The tea?"

"Yes, the tea. If you would go and make us a

cup of tea, that would be lovely. There's a tin of shortbread in the larder. Organic, quite delicious. I would go myself but, as you're here..."

Judy got up and walked out into the hall, as there didn't seem to be anything else to do. No way was she going to call the police. To the right was the front door. She *could* just walk through it, see if her shopping was still on the pavement somewhere, and go home. She stood for a moment, then turned left and went into the kitchen to put the kettle on and dig out the shortbread.

When she returned, carefully balancing mugs, teapot, milk, sugar and shortbread on a rather small tray, Mr Balderson looked at her smiling.

"Well, well, you decided to stay. Is Freddie Barnes on his way?"

"You mean the policeman? No, I haven't rung him … yet," she added, just to be on the safe side.

Mr Balderson walked over to the grate where Judy had put down the tea tray.

"Milk? Sugar?"

"Neither."

"Ah, I'm just the same." He gave Judy her mug

and then sat down himself in front of the fire. He took a sip of his tea.

"Very nice, thank you. Now where had I got to?" He looked into the fire and started to speak in a quiet, melodious voice as though he was continuing a conversation with himself that had been interrupted when Judy came back into the room.

"It is All Hallows' Eve. I call in Alcibiades so that he won't get into trouble – it's a dangerous night for cats in more ways than one – and I leave the door ajar. Why did I do that? An interesting question. Then over my threshold, uninvited and in silence, steps a young person, hunted and alone. At her heels, a couple of boys, the stupid sort, baying for blood. They run off – no mystery there, at least. Nastiness and cowardice: two sides of the same coin. The young person, confronted by an old one-eyed man in a coffin, does not say, "eek," or, "ewww," or have hysterics. And then, given the choice to go or stay, she stays. What shall we make of that? It is clear enough, I think. When she stands in the hall and looks at the front door, she has no particular reason to go through it. In her mind no kindly voices call;

nothing and nobody beckons to her on the other side of that door. No worried parents, no carefree friends in fancy dress wondering where she's got to. Not even a pet dog whining for its supper. Why should she leave?"

Judy felt as though she might cry. This feeling took her by surprise – she hadn't allowed herself to cry for a long time. But the odd old man had got straight under her skin, and it wasn't a nice feeling. "You don't know anything about me," she said.

The blue eye looked at her.

"We all know a great deal about one other, if we take the time to think about it. But of course you don't have to tell me anything. We can talk about the weather, or sing something, or tell each other stories. Or, best of all, we can just say nothing and drink our tea."

There was a long silence. They drank their tea. The strange figure in the armchair, his big slippered feet stretched out towards the fire, didn't seem to be waiting for anything in particular. He might have even forgotten that she was there.

Then Judy started to speak. For some reason

telling him things didn't seem like breaking faith with her father. Perhaps she had simply been alone for too long, or was just too tired, but once she started it was hard to stop. She spoke about her dad, about being alone on the narrowboat, forging her father's signature, lying to everybody all the time. She even spoke about Mr Greaves and how he was a nice man. Mr Balderson made small quiet noises sometimes or chuckled at something he thought was particularly funny, like Tyler falling into the canal. And he was very interested in William.

"Ah, the tree," he said. "The tree and the boy." He nodded his head to something that he seemed to understand that Judy did not.

By the time she was finished, Judy wasn't sitting on the sofa any more; she was half-lying, with her head on the armrest and her legs curled up under her. She was very tired.

"So that's it," she mumbled. "He's been gone for months. Any day now they'll be on to me, and cart me off to a care home. You might as well ring your policeman friend and get it over and done with. That's what grown-ups do."

"However, I haven't grown up," said Mr Balderson lightly. "Never got round to it. And if you thought I *had*, you wouldn't have told me in the first place."

Judy stared at him. The single eye stared back. He was right, of course. She had known straight away he wasn't a normal grown-up – they didn't sleep in coffins for a start – and this wasn't a normal place. In here you didn't have to choose between lying and being pushed around by people to whom you were a "case". People who said they knew what was best for you without knowing anything about you.

Then Mr Balderson leaned back, and his eye swivelled up towards the ceiling.

"So things are on the move. Such a storm, it was only to be expected…" he murmured. Then he linked his long fingers, cracked his knuckles, stood up and, stepping over the tea mug that he had put down on the floor, walked to the living room door. He threw it open and said,

"Farewell, *adieu*, *bon chance*…"

Judy stood up. She found that she didn't want to go. Now that she had finally talked to someone, she would have been quite happy to stay peacefully on the sofa, drinking tea and not having to deal with her life all on her own.

"Goodbye," he went on. "Off you go, time for bed, school tomorrow, and all that stuff. Josh and Tyler are but the fleeting memory of a dream."

"I don't care about them," said Judy. She stood up and walked into the hall. With her back to Mr Balderson she said stiffly, "Thank you for the tea."

"Miss Azad, one moment." Judy turned round, and with her back to the front door she met his gaze, her face blank and closed.

Mr Balderson went on. "I must ask you to understand that I have no help to offer you at this moment. Not the kind of help that waves a magic wand over your worries. That is not how this tale unfolds. Now you must walk back out into your life. This was a moment of sanctuary, not a solution."

He looked down at her, and Judy's face softened. Then he added,

"However, we are certainly at the beginning of *something*. You may be sure of that." Mr Balderson turned away and disappeared in the direction of the kitchen, calling quietly, "Alcibiades, you rogue, you snob, you high-stepping, self-regarding, preening, narcissistic jackanapes, come here. We have some more thinking to do."

Judy walked home through the deserted lamplit streets. She found her shopping where she had dropped it, or most of it anyway. Some of it had spilled out on to the pavement and got trodden on, but at least it hadn't been got at by rats or stray cats.

"Why did I do all that talking?" she said, half-aloud, as she turned into Canal Street. For a while, sitting on that sofa, she had felt something let go inside her, as though a tightly stretched cable had suddenly slackened. *I'd think he'd slipped something into the tea if I hadn't made it myself*, she thought. But telling the whole story had helped her get clear about one thing – she wasn't giving up just yet. She had been on the point of going to someone and saying that she was all alone, her father had gone off and left her, that she needed help. The meeting with Mr Balderson had been a stroke of luck, really. If he hadn't basically chucked her out of the house – if he had been a normal sort of adult, or one of

55

those supernormals you met all the time at school who nodded and smiled and understood everything and then wrote reports and assessments about you that ruined your life – then she would be on her way to some institution right now. As it was, she had got it off her chest without paying the price.

And now it was very late, well after midnight. She turned on to the towpath, and came to the narrowboat. The moon had set and only a dim park lamp lit the little door into the deckhouse. Inside the air was chilly and damp. She never left a heater on when she wasn't there. Her father had left behind lots of money and a cash card for her, and for a while she had felt really rich. But after all this time she was beginning to wonder how she could make it last. She lit the gas heater, and thought about boiling up some water and filling a hot-water bottle, but she couldn't be bothered. She undressed and crept shivering into her bunk, rubbing her feet together until they got a little warmer. She tried hard not to think too much about her father – what could have happened, where he could be. During the day it was easier, but at night, before sleep came, it was practically impossible. She couldn't go on denying what was staring her in the face. That for every day that passed, the odds that something had gone seriously wrong were increasing, and all she could do was wait while disaster rushed towards her like a boulder bouncing down a hill. *Think about something else*, she told herself. She chose Russell's paradox – that was a good one.

"Is the set of all sets that are members of themselves a member of itself?" she said aloud, and by trying to make sense of it she was soon asleep.

Much later, William woke. He could hear dance music thumping right through the house, so he knew his mother wouldn't be back yet. He turned on the light and sat down at his table, opening his notebook. He wrote and drew a picture of a monster, and a Roman soldier. Then he heard the street door open, and his mother coming up the stairs. She stumbled and said a rude word. He knew that she would probably go straight to her room, because she never felt very well after she had been out with Jerry, but he turned the light out and went back to bed anyway, just to be on the safe side.

3

Judy had been keeping her head down. There was no more trouble from Tyler and Josh. She had heard in school that Josh was moving to another part of town, and apparently Tyler never went out after dark at all.

She had a bit of a scare when her maths teacher said that he was thinking of getting her some extra maths teaching, and he would talk to her father about it, but she managed to fix that by very carefully making some ridiculous mistakes in her end-of-term exam, and even leaving a couple of questions unanswered. It was brilliant; just enough to get the pressure off, but not bad enough to start worrying people. The business of keeping up appearances had been a game at the beginning; outsmarting everybody was fun. But it's tiring being on your guard all the time, and the hardest thing is being on your guard against the dark thoughts – the little voice that whispers, *Something has gone wrong. He may never come back.*

The end of term brought some relief from the lies and the forged notes. Judy had the whole Christmas holidays ahead of her and she wouldn't have to worry about parents' meetings and end-of-term plays. But not being in school also made it harder to ignore that little voice. So Judy kept herself busy on the narrowboat, doing stuff that needed doing – like taking the generator apart and greasing the bearings and finding places indoors for some of the more sensitive pot plants that struggled in the cold weather. She had plenty to read, and was playing chess on her computer with someone in New Zealand who was much better than her and beat her every time. Trouble was, it didn't take long for Judy to run out of ideas to keep boredom and worry at bay. Most of the time she ended up lying on her back on her bed, staring at the ceiling. One afternoon she was doing just that; the pale winter sun was already on its way down on the other side of the canal, and was shooting its last few arrows of light through the window of the narrowboat, illuminating a shelf of books that were mostly her father's difficult textbooks and favourite poetry. As she followed the light with her eyes she saw something sticking up from one of them – a marker of some kind. She reached up and took down the book – an anthology of poetry – and, wondering which poem he'd been reading, opened it at the marked page.

It was a poem called "The Thousandth Man" and before she could read it, Judy saw that the book marker was an envelope, the edge ragged where it had been torn open. The envelope was addressed to her father – it had once contained the famous letter from Rashid that had sent him away from her. There was no letter inside now; her father had burnt that, Judy remembered. She turned the envelope over in her hands. Along the top on the back was a sender's address, but most of it was torn off. She could make out a postcode, though, and part of the name of a town or district. *A name, a number, a real place.* Judy thought of her father in Sweden, and for some reason this cheered her up a bit. After all, Sweden wasn't on the other side of the world. It wasn't Australia, or anything.

Quite suddenly she decided to get the place ready for Christmas, and she pulled out the decorations so she could string the fairy lights along the deck and hang tinsel in the bay tree. While she did, she daydreamed. In one of her daydreams she was sitting listening to the radio on Christmas Eve – the carol service from King's, perhaps – and she heard a thump as someone jumped on to the houseboat, and a voice called, "Jude, Jude, put the kettle on. I am very much in need of some refreshment," in that daft voice that her father put on when he was pretending to be upper class. She had decided that she would definitely not throw herself at him and hug him but when he came in she would be cool and dignified, and would say, "What took you so long?" Then he would explain everything and say that there was no one in this whole wide world who had a daughter who would do for him what she had done – wait, stick it out, and trust that everything would be OK. Then she would hug him. After that, in her story, they decided to have a proper English Christmas, with turkey and crackers and silly hats, and hang up a stocking over the stove to see if Santa Claus could squeeze himself down the stovepipe. And on Christmas day it would snow a bit, and they would go for a walk along the canal and he would say, "You see, I ordered Christmas, and it has been delivered."

A few days before Christmas, when William came home after a visit to the museum, to look yet again at the Roman and early English artefacts that had been dug up in the local area, he found a note from his mum on the kitchen table.

William, guess what? it said,

Jerry had a big win at Doncaster and we're off to Spain for a holiday. I've been feeling a bit off lately, so it should do me a bit of good. I know you won't mind.

I'll ring Nan and tell her to come and get you. I bet you'll have a great Christmas.

See you, love Mum.

William *didn't* mind, not really. Christmas wasn't something he looked forward to very much. The museum was always closed, there was an awful lot of shouting and fighting out in the street, even people being sick on the pavement, but the worst thing was that his mum usually came back from some party feeling very odd and wobbling about. Once she had put on some loud music and made him dance with her. He waited for Nan to call, but she didn't: not that day, and not the next day either. So he found her number written on the wall in the hall, and rang her. There was an answering machine. "This is Marjorie Parkinson, "Nan's voice said, "I can't answer right now, so please leave a message." William didn't leave a message, he didn't have time to think of what to say, but he knew where Nan lived so he took the number seventeen bus and got off at her street. He went up her little garden path and rang the bell. There was no answer.

"Hello, William, have you come to see your nan?" It was the woman who lived next door. She had come up her own path with her shopping bags. "Haven't you heard, she's in the infirmary, poor dear, had a bad fall, and they're worried about her heart on top of it all. She's in ward nine, but I think you'd better give her a few days before you visit."

William said thank you, and that he would give her a few days. Then he went home.

So Christmas came and went, and it meant very little to Judy or William. For Judy, it meant some nice music on the radio and a cheery greeting from the chess player in New Zealand, a day early of course. William stayed in too, sorting his collection and eating crisps and drinking coke. He didn't dare go outside.

And soon it was New Year's Eve. Judy was on her bunk reading Boole's *Laws of Thought*, which was a tough enough read to take anyone's mind off their worries. It had been a cold day, with heavy frost on the way, but Judy had lit the stove when she got up that morning, so it was warm and comfy in the boat. For the first time in ages Judy felt herself relax. And then she heard it: the thump of someone stepping on to the stern deck. For a moment she didn't move. She just waited, head down over her book, her hair draped around it like a curtain. But her heart started beating like a drum, while joy and relief gathered themselves to engulf her. The bit about being cool was going to be much, much harder than she expected. Then there was a knock at the door, and a man's voice called, "Hello, is there anyone at home?" Judy's head sank down on to her book. She recognized the voice instantly. It was Mr Greaves. She held her breath, silently begging him to please, please go away, but the knock came again. "Hello…?" and the little brass doorknob turned. Stooping low, Mr Greaves let himself in.

"Ah, there you are. I'm so sorry to intrude, Judy, but there was no answer, and I saw the smoke from the chimney so I thought something might have happened to you."

Judy said nothing. She sat up and slid her legs over the side of the bunk.

"Well, I must say, what a pleasant little home. Sorry to disturb your reading. School project?" he asked, peering through his spectacles at the book that still lay on Judy's pillow.

"Oh … the *Laws of Thought*. Not exactly

homework then. Beyond me, I'm afraid. Actually, I came here for a little chat with your father. I thought this might be better, since he seems to find it hard to get away… Do you mind if I sit down for a moment?" he added, turning away from the bunk and sliding in behind the table to sit on the bench. Judy took a deep breath.

"Dad's not here just now. He had a bit of business up North – he was here for Christmas, of course." Even to her, the lie sounded thin and tired.

Mr Greaves looked straight at her, and then it was upon her, the thing she had been dreading all this time.

"He wasn't here for Christmas, Judy," Mr Greaves said plainly. "Maybe you don't know where he is, maybe you *do* know but aren't saying. The point is that you have been lying about this for a long time, and it can't go on."

Judy almost gave in. Mr Greaves knew anyway, why go on with it? She opened her mouth to speak. Then she shut it again. It wasn't just about her. The questions would start – about her father, and Rashid. She might ruin everything.

"I'm not lying, he'll be back soon."

Mr Greaves sighed and shook his head. "Judy, you are one of the brightest pupils I have ever come across." He paused while his eyes moved to the book lying on her bunk. "So perhaps you can explain why there are no shoes larger than size six over there by the door, no overcoat on the peg in spite of the winter weather, only one bed made up, only one teacup on the draining board, and why there is nothing, nothing at all in this little space that suggests an adult lives here. Unless your father is a ghost."

Judy jumped up, hit the table with the flat of her hand.

"A ghost?" she shouted. "He's alive and he'll come back soon, he promised, you—" and she used a word that in school would have got her into a great deal of trouble. But Mr Greaves was different.

"Oh dear, I'm so sorry. What a stupid thing to say. It was just a form of words. Of course he's alive. But please, Judy, I need you to tell me what's going on. Then perhaps I can just go home for my tea."

"No."

Mr Greaves wrinkled his brow.

"Judy, I can bend rules. In fact, I spend a lot of my time doing just that. But I can't deliberately break them. I'll lose my job."

"So that's what this is about – your stinking job?"

"That's not fair, Judy, not fair at all. Even if I do lose my job, I'll be replaced by someone who is a lot less of a rule-bender than I am, so it won't help you one bit. Some people have a bad impression of the social services, but I know a very kind and thoughtful man; we've been friends for years. He has done a lot of good for a lot of people, and I am going to talk to him. I have to."

"You'll have me put into a care home?"

"For a short while, perhaps. It won't be hard to find a foster home for someone like you; there'll be plenty of takers. And they'll be trying all the time to get you back with your father."

"I know all about foster homes, my mum told me. She said she lived in hell until she was seventeen and got away. If Dad hadn't come along…"

"Ah, I see, there is a background to all this. Listen, Judy, you must not give up hope. There is so much you could do and be. You will grow up, and your life can be anything you make it. I mean it; it's not just words. There is always a way. I wouldn't be doing this job if I didn't believe that. You just have to take your life into your own hands."

Later, there would many evenings when Mr Greaves sat in his book-lined study and regretted his last words to Judy; because when the kind friend of his came round to fetch her, she was gone. The police were informed, of course, and Judy's photograph was added to the other photographs of missing children that they had in their files and on posters that hung in various public places around the town. There were a lot of photographs – there always are. People just disappear. Sometimes they want to, sometimes they don't … but they are still gone. There are tears of loss and sorrow for some of them, and for others, nothing at all.

4

When Mr Greaves had gone, Judy sat for a long time on the edge of her bunk, staring at the floor. It was time to leave. She had absolutely nowhere to go, but that wasn't what bothered her most. Just one more day, and he might come home, or there at least might be a postcard or a letter. She had promised to wait.

But it had gone on too long. To stay here and be dragged into the system, with people checking everything, asking questions, investigating her father, and then to live the kind of life that had just about destroyed her mum… It was impossible. In a day or two at the most the "nice friend" of Mr Greaves would come, all full of smiles and kind words, but if Judy put up a fight those kind words wouldn't stop the nice friend from fetching a couple of policemen. She had to go. Dad would understand. He would have to understand.

Once Judy had made the decision, she realized that she had to get moving or she would end up sitting there staring at the wall until they came for her. She stood up and looked around. The November cactus on the window shelf would have to go outside again and take its chances with the other plants. She made a mental list of what she needed to do: disconnect the generator, empty the fresh-water tank. What to take, what to leave behind? She pulled a holdall out from under the bench and began to throw things into it. Books, clothes, towel and washbag… The holdall now weighed a ton, and she tipped everything out on to the bunk and started again. Toothbrush, definitely. Sleeping bag, waterproof coat, clothes – warm ones – torch, pencil and paper, one book only … or maybe two. She took the cash card from its safe place, but she knew that she would have to empty the account and chuck the card as soon as possible; everyone knew it was dead easy to trace transactions. Lastly:

passport. She zipped up the holdall and stared at the little living space still filled with most of her stuff. She had often been lonely since her father went, but just as often comfy and peaceful, listening to the radio or reading, or just lying on her bed and thinking. There were some things about living like this that weren't much fun – dealing with the portable loo was one of them – but mostly it was nice. Really nice.

She took a last look around, found a pen and some paper, sat at the table and began to write. *Dear Dad,*

I promised I would wait, but you didn't come back. You didn't even send a message. If you ever see this…

She looked at what she'd written and scribbled it out viciously again and again, almost tearing a hole in the paper. "If you ever see this…" *If?* The thought was unbearable, that he might not ever come back. She tore up the note and took another sheet of paper, writing, *When you see this, you'll have to come and look for me. I have to go now. I'm sorry. Love, Judy.*

Turning off the light, Judy climbed out on to the

stern deck, locked the door and hid the key. As the winter evening settled down around her she shivered, stepped off the narrowboat and walked away.

Where to go? She was free to go anywhere. After only a hundred metres Judy sat down on a bench, while the lamps that illuminated the towpath for evening strollers flickered into life. She remembered once when she was younger being very cross when her father had forbidden her to stay out late with some friends.

"I have no freedom!" she had wailed.

"Freedom is not all it's cracked up to be, Judy," her father had said. "Just imagine nobody to tell you what to do, nobody to care for you or need you. And no love, of course. Freedom is rather hard work, confusing and tiresome, I would say."

A line popped into her head: *Freedom's just another word for nothing left to lose*. It was from a song that her mother used to sing before she got ill, when she was happy. Well, now Judy knew what it meant. She looked back along the towpath to where the narrowboat lay moored, faintly lit by one of the park lamps. Was she doing the right thing?

Then she saw a man standing on the towpath trying to peer through the window of the narrowboat. For a split-second her heart missed a beat, but he was nothing like her father. Too short, for a start. He was wearing a half-length overcoat, and a long scarf wound at least twice round his neck. As he moved towards the stern of the houseboat she could see that he walked with difficulty, dragging his left leg. He stepped on to the boat, and seemed to be trying the handle of the door. That was it then. Mr Greaves hadn't wasted any time at all; he must have suspected she would do a bunk. She had to get out of town as quickly as possible. Down to the bus station. She could buy a ticket to … anywhere, it didn't matter.

Half-walking, half-running, she left. Just outside the park entrance she saw a small car parked. Although she was in a serious hurry, she couldn't help noticing the digits on the number plate – the fifteenth number in the Fibonacci series, and the product of two prime numbers: 377.

Back at the houseboat the man frowned in

74

annoyance. It seemed she wasn't at home. He looked around, and saw a slight figure carrying a bag hurrying out of the park gates. He jumped awkwardly down from the houseboat, hindered by his leg, and started off towards his car.

The bus station was near the town centre, one of those modern travel centres with big sliding entrance doors and a ticket office, and lots of bays for local buses and long-distance coaches. There was quite an evening crowd, although the worst of the rush hour was over, and there were a fair number of people who weren't going anywhere – groups of young people, and homeless people pretending not to look for somewhere to sleep for the night or rooting for cans in the bins. There was a lot of litter and the occasional dirty pigeon. Judy wandered along the big curved concourse lugging her bag and reading the screens above each bay that displayed the destination of the bus. She had no particular place to go, but she had to make up her mind somehow. She decided on a town that was right on the other side of the country, by the sea. If worst came to worst she could always find somewhere to sleep on the beach, she thought. Perhaps she could live under an upturned boat, or in an old beach hut, and listen to the waves and look for cockles and winkles. The thought cheered her up a bit. She went into the ticket office, studied the timetables, and saw that she had a long wait ahead: over two hours. She bought a packet of crisps and a fizzy drink, a sandwich for later and a magazine, and looked around for the least uncomfortable bench, but most of the benches were already occupied by people who seemed to be preparing for a long stay. Judy looked towards the sliding entrance doors, thinking that it might be nicer to sit outside at least until it got too cold, and what she saw gave her a horrible shock: just inside the doors a man was standing staring intently about, a short man with a calf-length coat and scarf. The man who'd come to their boat. And now he had seen her. He started hurrying towards her, hampered by his leg. Judy picked up her bag and ran.

She ran until she was sure she had given him the slip, then slowed to a walk on a well-lit street near the town centre. She bought a paper mug of tea from a street vendor, ate her sandwich, and wandered round the shopping mall until it closed. The pavements were still full of people heading home or making their way to a cinema or restaurant or pub. Judy looked at her watch. In ten minutes the bus would leave; surely that man had gone home by now, to write his report and have his supper? But once she'd made her way back to the bus station, she saw that he hadn't. Moving carefully and making sure that she was masked as much as possible by passers-by, she spotted a small car parked on a double yellow line right in front of the main entrance, and made out the number plate: 377. She was going to miss the bus. And it looked as though she would be spending the night in a skip or a doorway, unless she could come up with a better option. She stood sipping her tea and thinking about it. There was only one person whom she could possibly turn to, and that was the strange person whom she had met at Halloween – the one who slept in a coffin. But he had been pretty clear about one thing. She had to make her own way. What was it he had said? *This is a moment of sanctuary, not a solution*. She gave up the idea of going to knock on his door.

So where do you sleep when you're out on the street? she thought. She had seen people in sleeping bags on the pavement lots of times; anybody who lived in a big city was used to that kind of thing. But now that she was one of them herself, she didn't really know what to do. You had to be pretty sure of yourself or pretty desperate to just lie down on the pavement or in a doorway, even if you weren't looking over your shoulder all the time and expecting to be followed.

She went to the public library, an old stone building with a pillared portico, but there were already a least three bundles of old clothes with people in them, lying on cardboard. Beside one of them was a dog that lifted its head and growled when she came up the steps. An alleyway between a corner shop and a pub looked promising, but the waste bins were full to overflowing, and the ground was sticky with muck. The gates of a small park were locked, though she could easily have climbed over them if she hadn't heard the sounds of angry voices coming from inside.

Judy leaned against a shop window on a well-lit street, and put her bag down beside her. She was tired and it wasn't easy to stay cheerful. She had to fight to stop herself from just going back to the houseboat, getting some sleep, and then turning herself in the next morning. She felt like a criminal who had given up running.

"Great," she said aloud. She leaned her head against the window frame and closed her eyes.

"Don't sit around, girl, you'll fall asleep."

When Judy opened her eyes there was a woman standing in front of her. She looked immensely stout at first sight, but then Judy saw that she was wearing layers and layers of clothing under a grimy coat, and that her face and hands were thin. She had long uncombed hair.

Judy stood up.

"I'm just resting. If this is your place, I'll move."

The woman snorted.

"Run off, have you? And just a kid. No, it's not my place, but I'm telling you to get moving, and keep moving. That's the rule for kids like you. That's the way to stay safe. Walk the night, sleep the day."

And she shuffled off round the corner. Judy heard her greet someone with a gritty laugh, then her voice faded into the night.

So Judy walked. The hours passed unbearably slowly. Midnight, one, two. It seemed like daybreak simply wouldn't come. Squatting with her back to the chain-link fence surrounding a building site, she stared eastward at the orange-grey night sky and begged it to lighten. All she wanted was a little streak of red to tell her that a day would come. But it didn't happen. She got up and walked on.

5

In the bluish light of daybreak, Andrew Balderson was in the kitchen preparing Alcibiades' breakfast. He was wearing a blouse and a skirt that reached to mid-calf, a wide one with a nice floral pattern. He had never been one for tight skirts. One of the marvellous things about women's clothing was the freedom of leg movement, the circulation of the air. Such a shame, really, that history had for some reason come down on the side of trousers for menfolk. The Greeks and Romans thought it was mad and uncivilized – they used to laugh at the trousered Gauls. And as for colour, and the chance to express some artistic sensibility, who on earth had decided that that was against the rules? If a banker or a businessman turned up for work in a colourful dress made by some famous fashion designer then they would lose their job immediately, although that applied to women too, for goodness' sake – they all had to wear grey suits nowadays. Why wasn't it the other way around? Today he had made a nice turban from a piece of Indian silk that was very colourful and included sequins among other things, and for good measure he had stuck a marigold, one of the last still standing in the garden, behind his left ear. On his feet were a pair of sheepskin slippers, not pretty at all, but so very, very comfortable.

"However," said Mr Balderson, addressing Alcibiades who had jumped on to the kitchen table and was eyeing him balefully, "I must now slip into something less comfortable and be on my way. The time has come. And you, old friend, will march off to Mrs Hodges' as usual and grow fat on whipped cream and titbits."

He was in a hurry, which was unusual. He had decided many years ago not to hurry any more, on the *Alice in Wonderland* principle that the faster you went the more you stayed in the same place, but now, as he left his house, he moved surprisingly quickly, with a long, loping, tireless gait that would have suited a hunter on the savannah or a herdsman on the steppe. He seemed incongruous in the narrow streets and run-down buildings of the old part of the city. Stopping in front of a pair of tall garage doors, with dirty green paint peeling off them in thin slivers, he listened to the screech of a handheld grinder that could be heard from inside. There was a smaller door in the wall to the side of the garage entrance, with a grubby faded notice that said "G.Wayland Smith, Mechanic." Mr Balderson tried the handle, and then started beating at the door with the flat of his hand and roaring, "Georgie? Georgie, my lad, let me in. It's Andy." After a while the grinder fell silent and Mr Balderson shouted once more. "Georgie, open up, will you?"

After a moment there was the sound of someone fiddling with the catch, and the door opened a little to reveal a pair of very suspicious eyes in a pinched and extremely dirty face. The face had obviously been wearing goggles, because the skin was clean around the eyes, giving the impression of a wizened monkey. Then the door was opened properly and a small man in overalls that had once been blue said, "Oh, it's you. Didn't expect you. I've got a rush job on." After looking carefully up and down the street he went on.

"In with you then. Come for him, have you? He's filled up and I gone over him, shouldn't have any trouble. Transmission's a bit dodgy, but you know that already. I'll get the keys." He disappeared into a cubby-hole that could have been an office if it wasn't completely overflowing with bits of engines, batteries, chargers, washers and bolts and gaskets and sparking plugs, and rooted around like a hog in a turnip field muttering, "In here somewhere…" There were two vehicles in the large space. One of them was a very shiny luxury car that looked absolutely perfect, with dazzling bodywork and aluminium wheels. But the grinder was on the floor beside it, and the bonnet was open and the front end was jacked up. The other vehicle was a camper, or perhaps you could call it a motorized caravan. It wasn't just a van anyway, it was built on the chassis of a small truck, with flat sides, and windows, and a door, and a flat roof with a low rail round it. There was a ladder fixed to the back. Georgie returned from his search, proudly dangling a set of car keys.

Mr Balderson smiled and gave the side of the camper a friendly pat.

"Right, Aristeas," he said. "It is time for us be on the move again. I feel it strongly."

He opened the cab door and climbed in behind the wheel, then rolled down the window and leaning out he called,

"Thanks, Georgie. Don't do anything I wouldn't do."

"Not a chance," came the reply, "I can't think of anything."

Mr Balderson chuckled and gunned the engine, which made a satisfying dieselly roar in the confines of the garage. And he was off.

It was starting to rain. Judy walked the wet pavements in the grey drizzling beginning of what would pass for daylight in an hour or so. There were already people about – mostly women, huddled and hurrying, on their way home from their unseen night work cleaning offices and shopping malls for the bright and shiny young women and the men with polished shoes who would arrive later to do … whatever it is they do.

In the light of day – even a grey, damp day – things look different. Judy was able to start thinking again, in spite of her exhaustion. Living like a vagabond wasn't as easy as it looked. Her daydream about living under a boat on the beach was very romantic, very sad and, she now realized, very stupid. There was only one thing she really *wanted* to do, and that was find her father, or at least find out what had happened to him. She had promised to wait. She had promised not to send emails and phone messages. But she hadn't promised not to go after him. And there was only one possible place to start looking. She would have to get to Sweden, to the place that letter came from.

It would be a quest, an adventure, and it would be her own choice, not something that just happened. It was a mad idea, but she didn't care – she was free to do anything she wanted, and if she never got there, what did it matter? At least she would try. At least she could answer the question, "What are you doing?" with, "I am looking for my father," instead of, "Nothing in particular." She found herself standing on the corner of a big road that was starting to fill up with morning traffic. She headed left in the direction of the train station.

Once there, Judy checked out train times, and ferry crossings to the continent. But, apart from the fact that it was all incredibly expensive, she wasn't even sure that they would sell her a ticket because of her age. She needed a better plan. Lots of people her age managed to get into England in the backs of lorries, or hanging underneath them or something, so how hard could it be to get out? So she decided to walk out of town to the big service station on the bypass and try to sneak on to a lorry going to the docks. At least she had managed to brush her teeth in the train station toilets. Brushing your teeth always gives you a more positive feeling about life. She hoisted her bag on to her shoulder and started off, following the signs that would eventually take her on to the main road out of town. The rain had let up a bit, but the tires of passing cars still hissed along the rain-soaked streets and threw spray from the puddles. One of the cars slowed down as it drove past her, and the driver looked out at her with a rather creepy smile on his face. This wasn't a very nice part of town – everybody knew that – and she was glad that it was now daytime. She walked on up a long street that at this time of morning was fairly deserted, although Judy knew that at night there were a lot of pubs and clubs open. It was one of those streets that would definitely have got her a lecture about freedom if her father ever heard she had been there. Now there were only the betting shops open, that and a couple of cafés.

A large van drove past and she jumped aside to avoid getting her shoes splashed, watching as the van slowed down and stopped. It wasn't a delivery van, but some kind of mobile home. Judy kept walking, keeping a wary eye on it. It wasn't a posh shiny camper, the kind that comes out in the summer and goes to a nice resort on the French Riviera. It was more like the sort of thing that had been on the road for a long time. It looked very lived-in, and you couldn't help wondering what sort of people had lived in it, and what they had got up to. The cab door on the driver's side, which she couldn't see, slammed shut. Someone had got out. And there was no mistaking the tall figure who came round the front of the camper and stepped on to the pavement. Mr Balderson was wearing a wide-brimmed hat and a long overcoat that almost swept the ground.

"Well, well, wonders will never cease. There I was, off on a little jaunt, and what do I see? A small familiar personage hiking out of town – clearly on her way somewhere. Am I wrong?"

"No, actually."

"I thought not, I rarely am. And breakfast? What about breakfast?"

"I'm not particularly hungry." This was a complete lie. She had suddenly realized that she was absolutely starving.

"Incredible. You must be made of stern stuff. Hardly human. I myself am peckish. I don't suppose I could persuade you to join me in a cup of tea, before we go our different ways?"

Judy shrugged her shoulders.

"There's a place open just up here," said Mr Balderson, pointing up ahead.

Judy followed him into a small grimy café, with formica tables and plastic chairs, and they took a seat by the window. A surly waitress slouched over and asked them what they wanted. Mr Balderson ordered two mugs of tea, no sugar no milk, and asked Judy, "Do you want anything else? They have a bacon butty, I see."

"No thank you."

"Never mind, I'm going to have lots of toast and marmalade."

The tea came, in large mugs, and the toast and marmalade.

Mr Balderson started eating.

"So, where are you off to?" he asked

"I'm leaving the country. I'm going to look for my father."

"How exciting – an epic in the making. 'The Lay of Azad' or what about 'Judy's Saga'? Where are you going to look? No, don't tell me, I love to guess… Let me see… He leaned back in his chair and gazed at her. "Azad… Farsi, I think, or Persian as we used to say… Ah Persia, once so noble, the land of the Magi, of glorious poets and brilliant thinkers, but now" – he shook his head sadly – "a disturbed part of the world, no doubt about it. Yes, I'm definitely guessing Persia. The name, the looks, the hair, the eyes, the nose, the mathematics…"

Judy was offended. Not about the hair and the eyes, which she was secretly quite pleased with, but the nose, which was already showing signs of the eagle-like beakiness of her father's.

"How do you know that I like maths?"

"Well, goodness me, it stands to reason. Germany and music, Ireland and horses, France and food… Persia and algebra."

"That's not where I'm going."

"I was wrong! How unusual. So tell me, please, Miss Azad. I am so helplessly inquisitive, and you have eaten all my toast and marmalade."

Judy looked down at the table in surprise. It was true, she had.

"I'm going to Sweden," she said.

Mr Balderson's single eye widened and he clapped his hands together.

"Astounding! Extraordinary! Almost beyond belief!"

"What do you mean?"

"Well, I'm on my way there myself. Isn't that amazing? How lucky that I don't believe in coincidences, because if I did, this would be hard to swallow. But as it is, I have no doubt that the unseen pattern is being carefully woven by the fates – urd, verdandi, skuld – ha ha, we have caught a glimpse, a corner of the veil has briefly blown aside."

Mr Balderson had quite a lot more to say on the subject of patterns and fate, with quotations from poetry and ancient texts. He mentioned aetiology and serendipity and a number of other things that Judy was not at all clear about and wasn't really listening to. She looked out through the dirty café window misted with condensation streaming down the glass, and on to the bleak littered street and the stained brick buildings opposite. Was he really going to Sweden? Could coincidences like this really happen, or was something else going on that she didn't understand? Mr Balderson swivelled his eye, which had been pointing at the ceiling, back in her direction.

"It seems that our road is the same, at least for a while. Perhaps we are destined to be travelling companions."

"I'm not sure…" Judy began, but she was cut off in mid-sentence.

"Of course not, how could you be? Who is ever sure about anything? The people I have known who have been sure about things have been extremely boring and given to all sorts of odd behaviour, most of it not very nice. But the choice is yours." Judy acknowledged that Mr Balderson seemed to have an answer to everything. She wasn't sure that this was a good thing.

It was just like the first time they had met, when she had made the tea instead of walking out. But this time was deadly serious. A lot more serious than sitting on someone's sofa for an hour or two. If her Dad had been here… But he wasn't, that was the whole point, wasn't it? Now she had a real chance. Judy heard herself say,

"If you really are going there, then maybe…"

Mr Balderson stood up, reached into one of his

voluminous pockets for some money to leave on the table, and strode out of the café. Judy quickly gulped the last of her tea and followed him.

They drove through town. Judy said nothing. What was there to say? She was being driven somewhere by a person whom she knew practically nothing about, except that he was definitely not ordinary and possibly mad. Perhaps she should have been a lot more worried than she was. But she couldn't get away from the feeling that in this story, or on this quest or whatever it was, Mr Balderson was not playing the part of the baddy.

"So," said Mr Balderson, breaking into her thoughts "Where are we off to?" He spoke quite loudly, above the sound of the engine that was located under its cowling between the passenger seats.

Judy's heart skipped a beat.

"Well, Sweden…"

"Indeed. But Sweden is rather a large country, is it not? Long."

"There was a sender's address on the back of an envelope. The name of the town was half ripped off, but I saw the postcode. I remember it because the square root was a whole number."

"A whole number? You don't say. Very Pythagorean. We go right at the roundabout, for the docks; we'll worry about the rest later."

For a long time Judy had lived carefully, keeping everything under control. Then, after Mr Greaves' fateful visit, she had just run off with no proper plans or purpose. Now she *had* a purpose, but all there was to do was sit and watch the countryside, houses, fields and petrol stations fleeing past. She had been like a tightly wound spring, driving herself, but now she seemed to have snapped. Soon her eyelids grew as heavy as lead, her head fell backwards, and she sank into a comatose sleep.

6

Judy woke up as they drove into the huge ferry terminal and parked in a long queue of vehicles. As Mr Balderson got out to get the tickets organized, Judy looked out at the big ferry waiting to depart; this was the point of no return. She was off on a journey with no clear idea of what was at the end of it. But at least there was some hope that it would lead her to her father. When Mr Balderson returned and the camper van was rattling up a ramp into the clanging bowels of the ship, bullied into the right place on the car deck by a man in an orange safety vest, Judy started to speak.

"What if… I mean there is only a chance…"

"There is only…" replied Mr Balderson, "action,

or non-action. You have chosen action. That is enough. Do not act for the fruits of action, bound to the desire for a result. Just act. Let's go up on deck and observe the gulls," he added, as a great thundering *clang* announced that the bow doors were closing and the ferry was about to depart.

"But I do desire a result; I really do. What's wrong with that?" said Judy, as they climbed the stairs from the car-deck and emerged into the open air.

"Nothing is wrong with that, but it is neither here nor there. Meaningless. Inconsequential. We cannot possess the future. Only the present is truly ours."

They walked to the stern rail, shivering a bit in the wind that struck the slab-sided ferry as soon as it left the river-mouth. A big black-backed gull slid past on the updraft as the ferry hooted a mournful goodbye to England. Judy looked at the rapidly shrinking coastline, the high terminal building already small and insignificant and the cars like little toys. She saw a small blue car turn into the parking area, driving much too fast and coming to a sudden halt. The driver jumped out and stood very still. It was too far away to see any details, and of course at that distance she couldn't make out the number plate; but if it was Mr Greaves' very nice friend from the social services department then he was too late. She had escaped.

Afterwards, when Judy tried to remember her journey north, she would find it quite hard. All the everyday worries that had nagged at her for months had fallen away. Now as the distance from England increased, there were moments of near-panic about what she had got into, but mostly tiredness got the upper hand and she spent quite a lot of the time asleep. Even awake, she was constantly half dreaming. Aristeas the camper had rolled off the ferry in Holland, and between Rotterdam and Utrecht the traffic moved like some dense, viscous syrup, twelve lanes across and carpeted with huge lorries from every nation in Europe – Polish, Serbian, Czech, French, Spanish, German, Turkish, Bulgarian. Judy spent some time working out which of the number plates were prime numbers, but she lost interest after a while. The traffic was so slow that there was time to look into the cabs of the trucks on either side, as Aristeas painstakingly overtook them or was passed himself. In every one a long-distance traveller, resigned to their work. Sometimes their eyes met. Rarely, a faint smile. Once, even, a wink. At one point, when four lanes packed with traffic were supposed, in some miraculous way, to turn into two, Mr Balderson took his foot off the accelerator to let in a huge sixteen-wheeler from Rumania, and as the great beast squeezed in between the camper and the truck in front, a lazy, hairy hand appeared out of the side window and made a little gesture of thanks. Not a wave exactly, but pretty close. At last after seemingly endless miles, the traffic started flowing faster as it headed east. And then, as one motorway fed into the next, they veered north. Night fell, and the lanes of traffic became a serpent of light, red on one side, white on the other. Big blue and white motorway signs passed overhead for Berlin, Bremen, Oldenburg, Hamburg and Lubeck.

"Enough for today," announced Mr Balderson, and they pulled in to a big service station, with a huge parking area already filled with lorries. They found a space between two of them, and snuggled in like a kitten in a pride of lions. Mr Balderson turned off the engine. He clambered back between the front seats. In the camper it was all very snug. There was a little gas stove at the back, and a sink, and a couple of cupboards, two upholstered couches on either side of a little table, and above the driving seats an alcove with a wooden ladder leading up to it. Judy felt very much at home. It was all a lot smaller than the narrowboat, but had the same air of efficient use of space and simple living.

"I shall retire upstairs," said Mr Balderson, gesturing towards the little ladder. "The table folds down, and converts into a bed. There is a quilt and a pillow in the space under one of the couches." And without further ado he climbed up the ladder and into the alcove, politely drawing a little curtain that hid him from view. Judy worked out how to collapse the table, and turn the couch seats into a mattress. When the seat cushions were removed, she saw that the benches had hinged lids, making lockers for storage. In one of them were the water tank, some tools, and a mandolin. She opened the other one, and started back in shock. Someone was in there. Her first wild thought was that she had been horribly mistaken about nice Mr Balderson, but then she saw that in the bench locker, curled up and looking pale and tired, lay William Parkinson.

Judy stared unbelievingly. William lay on top of a rather grubby flowery quilt, eyes closed, mouth half-open. He opened his eyes – Judy noticed them for the first time, pale brown, or hazel perhaps, the irises large, the whites very white. He looked up at her.

"I fell asleep. Are you surprised to see me?"

"What do you think?" said Judy as she worked on composing herself.

William managed to sit up in the awkward space.

"I think you are surprised, and mostly not pleased. But you don't have to be angry. I thought I would hide and then when the van started moving I would come out and then I could come with you and talk about my find. If I had asked you, you would probably have said no."

Judy drew breath to get started on what she wanted to say to William Parkinson, but he went on,

"I know you don't want me to come. I can go now," he sighed. Judy found her voice.

"Go? Go where?"

"Go home. I bet there's a bus, and anyway I'm a good walker, Nan always says. Have we driven far?"

"Yes we have, William, we're in Germany."

"I've never been to Germany before."

"Well you have now. Get out of there, will you?"

William stood up and stepped out of his hiding place, looking around him. His eyes immediately fastened on one or two things that looked very interesting. On the shelf above the couch opposite him, for example, next to a brass telescope, was an odd little doll with small shells sewn on to it, and a piece of broken pottery decorated with what looked like dolphins. There were books, and pictures tacked to the walls, and a string of beads that hung from a peg together with a decorated leather belt and a wicked-looking knife. But there was no time to explore the camper, because Judy's eyebrows were flat-lining, her nostrils were bigger than usual, and her eyes definitely flashed. In fact she looked pretty dangerous, although William knew perfectly well that she wasn't really a dangerous person.

"William, you great twerp, you have messed everything up! You've got yourself smuggled out of the country and we'll have to get you back. I'll get pinched and Mr Balderson will probably go to jail for kidnapping. Everything's ruined. Oh my God, why didn't I just leave those two morons to get on with it?"

"Which two…? Oh, Josh and Tyler. But if you had left them to get on with it they would have taken my find, you know."

A solemn voice spoke from behind the alcove curtain, conjuring up in Judy a sudden memory of a school lesson about the tabernacle and Jehovah and the Ark of the Covenant.

"Indeed, and had you done as you say you would not be here either, Judy. Cause and effect, the butterfly flaps its wings on the other side of the world, and the storm breaks above our heads. The marvellous way of the world, its exciting unpredictability."

It was true. If she had walked away from the business with Josh and Tyler, she would never have ended up hiding in Mr Balderson's house, and … well, all the rest of it. She slumped on to the seat and rested her elbows on the little table, her head in her hands.

Mr Balderson's head stuck out from behind the curtain.

"There's always a saying to fit the occasion, I find. In this case I would opt for, 'You can't have your cake and eat it.'"

William had been observing the head that had appeared above them. Now he said, "Hello."

"Of course, you are William! What a pleasant surprise – are you joining us?" Mr Balderson chuckled happily.

"I wanted to talk about my find, and about the tree, but I fell asleep."

"I shall look forward to that," said Mr Balderson. But now something else had caught William's attention.

"Why have you only got one eye?"

"What a pleasure to talk to someone who says what he thinks, don't you agree, Judy?" was Mr Balderson's response.

"Did someone throw a stone at you? Some people throw quite badly. Not Judy though, she's very good at it."

"No, it wasn't a stone. It's a long story, William.

There was a price to pay, and I paid it."

"Was it something expensive?"

"Very expensive. Too expensive to be bought with money."

This was too much for Judy. She was trapped in a camper van in the middle of Europe with two people who were... Well, to call them odd was being kind.

"Please stop this," she yelped. "What are we going to do? William, how on earth did you find us and get in here?"

"I looked out of my window and I was just thinking about if you were my friend and there you were going into the café across the road, so I..."

"OK, I get it. And now your mother will be having hysterics and calling the police."

"No she won't."

"Of *course* she will."

"She's in Spain."

"Well, who are you staying with?"

"Nobody. My nan's in hospital, she fell down. I don't know anybody else."

"Well, this is all absolutely fascinating,"

105

interjected Mr Balderson. "We shall have lots to talk about tomorrow. I am looking forward to talking about your nan, William, and other things. The pattern is being woven, thread by thread. The journey has only just begun."

William wanted to ask about the threads and the pattern, but Mr Balderson's head had disappeared again.

"Shall I get back into the bench? You can pretend I'm not here." William looked uncertainly at Judy, who sighed loudly.

"Don't be stupid."

She folded down the table and organized the couch cushions, then took out her own sleeping bag and laid out the quilt and a pillow for William.

"Right, you're on this side. If you snore you can go up and sleep on the roof."

William crept under his quilt, and Judy turned off the ceiling lamp.

"How will I know if I'm snoring?"

"Don't worry, I'll let you know."

"I like being here, Judy."

"Shut up and go to sleep."

7

So William came along. What else was there to do? He had no passport, and they couldn't just put him on a boat. Besides, it seemed that nobody even had the faintest idea that he had left. Of course, that would change when his mother came home from Spain, or the school term started. Judy turned over various possibilities in her mind, but the main problem was that Mr Balderson was hopelessly uninterested in making any effort to get rid of William. Quite the opposite, in fact. Over their morning porridge, as the traffic thundered past on the motorway and a pale winter sun did its best to penetrate the low-lying mists of Northern Germany, he listened intently as William chattered about the great ash tree, and his mysterious find.

"Our fate is a kaleidoscope," he said, when William paused for breath. "All those little coloured pieces jumbled up, then a little twist and hey presto! The pattern appears. Each one of us is a little coloured piece. We all have our parts to play. Perhaps William here has the leading role? Is this really *his* story? Are you and I mere bit-players, Judy? Extras? Crowd scene? We do not know, we cannot say."

Judy took another spoonful of porridge. Normally she hated porridge, absolutely loathed it, but that might have been partly to do with her father, who said, *How could a country that produced Isaac Newton and trial by jury create this? It really is a blot on their copybook.* When she tried to refuse the porridge she had got a long harangue from Mr Balderson, who said that he had learned the true art of porridge-making from a crofter in the Western Isles, and that his porridge was a culinary masterpiece worthy of Escoffier, and that nobody who travelled in his camper van was permitted to refuse porridge, and generally speaking he had no truck with young people who didn't eat.

Actually, Judy found that piping hot porridge with syrup wasn't a totally ghastly experience.

She swallowed her mouthful. "If we are all just characters in a story, then who is telling it? Who is twisting the kaleidoscope?" she said to Mr Balderson, and he looked absolutely delighted. Sighing with pleasure, he leaned back against his seat cushion and took a sip of tea.

"Oh yes. One of the great questions. One of the *real* questions. One of the questions that has a thousand answers or none."

"Thanks, very enlightening."

"At your age, a touch less uppitiness would suit very nicely."

Judy looked down at her bowl. She knew that she was like that, making sarcastic remarks, and it wasn't one of the good things about her. If there were any good things.

"Sorry. But things just happen, don't they, one after another, in an endless line from the beginning. All these patterns and the warp and weft of fate…"

"Well, well, you *are* an old fogey, aren't you? The

whole business of life is just bits of stuff bumping into each other, is it? Like billiard balls?"

"Sort of, I suppose."

"Not many physicists would agree with you these days, but never mind that. What about this: to someone who is tone-deaf, a Bach cantata is just a long line of notes happening one after the other. Are you tone deaf, Judy, or can you hear the music? Do you even want to? And as for the composer, well, does it really matter? When you hear a wonderful piece of music – something that makes you happy and sad at the same time, something that makes the hair on the back of your neck stand on end – then the question of who or what made it is mere curiosity. And you know what they say about curiosity."

"*I* don't know," said William. He was looking a lot better than last night, but rather crumpled, and, thought Judy, not very clean. They would have to stop and at least buy him a toothbrush.

"It killed the cat," said Judy, and instantly regretted it.

"Whose cat?" asked William.

"Nobody's in particular."

"How can you kill nobody's cat?"

"It means that cats in general are curious, and being curious can get you into trouble."

"Cats aren't curious. Duck-billed platypuses are curious, though, they have beaks and fur and..."

Judy frowned.

"What...? Oh I see. There are two kinds of curious, William. One of them is... how things look to you, and the other is how you look at things, I suppose."

"Am *I* curious?"

"Definitely."

"Which kind?"

"Both."

"Will I die, then?"

"No, it only kills cats."

"But..."

"That's it, William. End of conversation."

William liked sitting in front. Judy had the passenger seat, but there was lots of space for him between the two front seats, because the cab was sort of on top of the engine, and the engine cowling

111

was there. He sat on it, on a pillow. It wasn't a proper seat, and there was no seatbelt. When he had asked about it, Mr Balderson said, "You can't have everything. We must take the rough with the smooth." Aristeas had a big wide windscreen, and William was perched quite high up, so he could see a lot. Mostly it was just cars and lorries and buses, with lines of trees and sometimes petrol stations at the side of the motorway, but sometimes you could see out over the flat countryside, where farmsteads with big roofs and low walls stood all alone in huge fields with only a few wind-bent trees for company. Enormous electricity pylons marched like an army of giants across the land, their tops seeming to touch the low purply-grey sky.

At around lunchtime it started to rain. Big trucks threw up great fountains of spray, the wipers went back and forth – *slash tick, slash tick* – and you couldn't see much except for the misty red spots that were the tail lights of the cars in front. It was warm in the cab, particularly for William on top of the engine. Judy had her feet up on the dashboard, and her eyes closed. William was just thinking that she looked all right – not *happy*, but all right – when he saw her eyebrows get closer to each other, and a wrinkle appear between them.

Judy *had* been all right, lulled half-asleep by the rhythm of the windscreen wipers and the warmth of the cab, until in an unguarded moment she had let herself start thinking about how many millions of vehicles were on the motorways of Europe at any one time, their average speed, their weight per axle, the mean distance from front to rear bumper, and about what would happen if the temperature suddenly dropped below zero, the road surface iced over, and the driver of some juggernaut stamped on his air-brakes and jack-knifed. Presumably there would be a multi-vehicle pile-up that stretched from Bilbao to Budapest. After all, it was the middle of winter, wasn't it? She opened her eyes, remembering the story she had told herself about her father jumping on to the deck on Christmas Eve and calling, "Jude, Jude…" She didn't know whether to laugh or cry. Nothing was real to her any more. She remembered suddenly a little talk that Mr Greaves had given in assembly about Macbeth.

He was always going on about Shakespeare. "Life, says Macbeth, is 'a tale told by an idiot, full of sound and fury, signifying nothing.'" But then he had said that Macbeth was very sad and depressed; that he had done some seriously bad stuff because he had believed what the weird sisters told him, and on top of that his wife had died. "So sometimes it feels as if nothing means anything," Mr Greaves had said. "But that doesn't mean it's true. The sun comes out, or someone smiles at you, and suddenly everything, *every little thing*, has significance. Remember that when you are feeling sad. And don't trust the weird sisters – they never tell you everything."

Judy looked across at William and Mr Balderson, who had exchanged his wide-brimmed slouch hat for a tasselled bright red fez, found a radio station he liked, and was thumping on the steering wheel in time to a rousing opera chorus. And here we are, thought Judy. *Da-da! The weird sisters*. She chuckled. Mr Balderson looked at her.

"Yes, marvellous isn't it? Fidelio!" Judy burst out in a peal of laughter. Mr Balderson smiled back at her happily.

"Luckily the left eye works. Driving on the right, you know."

Judy's laughter died a sudden death. She hadn't thought about that. He was half-blind! That didn't improve their chances of not becoming a statistic in the foreseeable future.

By teatime the rain had stopped. Mr Balderson swung off the motorway on to a slip road, and they drove for a long time down small straight roads lined with poplars and linden, through neat villages with red-brick houses whose roofs seemed almost to reach down to the ground, leaving hardly any room for the windows and doors. Mr Balderson seemed to be looking for something. The sun was already almost on the horizon. It managed to sneak a few rays under the clouds, making sudden flashes on windows and puddles. Then it was gone, and a gloomy dusk began to envelope the landscape.

"Here we are," he said, and they turned off on to what was not much more than a metalled track. It was obviously a campsite, but not a holiday camp, the kind with a reception desk and a shop selling food and sweets and gas cylinders and inflatable toys, and a shiny clean shower block. In among the trees, which stood quite far apart, the ground was covered with a thick layer of pine needles and rather a lot of the kind of rubbish that you don't want to look at too closely. The stuff that people leave because it's smelly or empty or both, and they don't want to have it in their cars and they can't be bothered to look for a bin. And, thought Judy as Mr Balderson manoeuvred the camper into a space that was reasonably clear of plastic bags and worse, they can't work out what it would look like if you multiplied it by a million.

"This is a nice spot," she muttered, and then regretted it. She had to stop trying to be smart and sarcastic all the time. She had to just let things be. That's what Mr Balderson did, William too for that matter. And there was no other way to survive this trip without going barking mad.

"The great thing about winter travel," said Mr Balderson, opening the driver's door and clambering out, "is that you usually have the place to yourself." Cold air streamed into the cab.

"Come out and stretch your legs."

"We'll have to find something for William," called Judy. "He'll freeze to death." She was pulling out a jumper from her holdall.

"Look in one of the cupboards."

Judy rooted around for a while. There was plenty to choose from. She found a woollen hat and a lined jacket, and took them to William who was already outside. He seemed cheerful enough, looking around, but his shoulders were hunched up and he was already shivering.

"Instinct for self-preservation: zero points," said Judy. "Put these on." The jacket hung down below his knees, but Judy rolled the sleeves up, and put the hat on his head. The long winter evening was morphing into night at last. Already the trunks of the trees were mere silhouettes against the evening sky, and in the fading light you had to walk carefully and keep your eyes on the ground to avoid stepping on something you didn't want to step on. Mr Balderson had disappeared.

"Come on, William, we have to move around."

They wandered for a bit, flapping their arms.

There wasn't much to see. The area was bigger than it had looked at first; there was a padlocked concrete hut which might once have housed proper bins, or even a toilet, and beyond it a few bedraggled bushes, and there was more of the site on the far side. But it was getting too dark to walk far, and they were about to turn back when they heard voices. Apparently they were not the only campers. Then they heard a laugh, a rumbly cheerful one that they knew well. They walked on, and on the other side of the bushes they saw a car parked some way off, with some people squatting round a very small smoky fire on the ground beside it. The largest person was Mr Balderson, but they couldn't make out much else. They walked forward and the mumble of voices stopped, but not before Judy had caught a word that gave her a jolt. Heads were turned towards them, and Mr Balderson stood up.

"Hello there, I was just having a little chat. As you see we are not quite alone here. Fellow-travellers." They were close enough now to see the motley assortment of clothes that the campers wore, but not much else. They were muffled up to the eyebrows against the chill of the night. A dark eye here, a bit of stubbly chin there, a wisp of hair escaping from a woman's shawl.

"Come and say hello," said Mr Balderson. Judy approached, but William stayed where he was.

"Come on, William," Judy said.

"No. I don't want to."

"Ah," said Mr Balderson. "Time to be getting to bed, I think. William looks like he needs to get his head down." He said a cheerful goodbye to the silent group, and started back to the camper. Judy didn't move. Had she heard right? Then a man stood up, pushing back the hood of a parka that had seen better days, and took a step towards her. He looked into her face and said,

"Good night, sleep well. I wish you a joyful end to your journey."

He spoke in perfect, beautiful Farsi. For a tiny moment it was as if her father was speaking to her, out of the mouth of a sad man in scuffed trainers and torn jeans. Judy was about to reply, but William was tugging at her arm. On the way back, picking their way among the rubbish, William said,

"Who were they?"

"Refugees, migrants, asylum seekers, how should I know?"

"Were they vermin?"

Judy stopped dead.

"What did you say?"

"Jerry, he's my mum's boyfriend, he says they're vermin. They come into the country and steal things and cheat and use up taxpayers' money. He says they take bread out of the mouths of proper Englishmen. That's stealing, isn't it?"

A calm and peaceful Judy could have taken a few deep breaths and given herself time to see the whole thing: who William was, how his life was. But she wasn't feeling calm and peaceful. She grabbed the lapels of his ridiculous oversized jacket and backed him up against a tree, with her face inches from his.

"Listen, you pathetic dope. Your teaching assistant and your so-called special needs and your psychologists cost the famous taxpayer around fifty thousand a year, I reckon. Most of the schools in England will do anything to get out of having you.

Does that make you vermin? And then there's me. I've only got a British passport because of my mum. My Dad's not English. So I'm vermin too. As for Mr Balderson, God knows what he is, but I bet he counts as vermin according to your Jerry. And right now, William, while we're on the subject of vermin, if I had to choose between you and a sewer-rat, I'd go for the rat."

Even as she spoke Judy knew that she was being viciously cruel, but she couldn't stop herself. William had his eyes tight shut, and now he started beating the back of his head rhythmically against the trunk of the tree. Judy let him go. He slid down inside the oversized jacket, which had snagged on the rough bark, and curled up in a ball at the bole of the tree. The jacket flopped down over his head, and in the gloom he might as well have been just another bit of rubbish. Judy looked down at him. Tears squeezed out from the corners of his tightly shut eyes. She'd never seen him do that before. It made her want to cry herself. She dropped to her knees.

"William, I'm sorry. I just think Jerry's wrong,

that's all. Nobody who is at the bottom of the heap should be called vermin. There are all sorts down at the bottom, but there are all sorts at the top too. And there are a thousand ways to cheat and lie that people use all the time, every day: poor, rich, English, foreign. It makes no odds; it's everybody. Rich people are big cheats, and poor people are small cheats."

"Like me, you mean. I'm a bad person." His voice was almost a whisper.

"No, no, no, that isn't what I meant at all. Honestly. Really. You don't cheat."

"But you said it was everybody."

"Almost everybody."

She leaned over and spoke, her mouth at his ear.

"William Parkinson, you are one of two people I know who is neither a cheat nor a liar."

William opened one eye.

"Are you the other one?"

Judy laughed and shook her head.

"No, William, I am not. I'm the biggest liar there is. I've been lying like anything for months – to everybody. But I need to stop now. I'll try to be more like you. Come on." She helped him up and brushed the pine needles off his jacket. They walked back towards the camper.

"Who's the other one, then?"

"Guess."

"Your dad."

"Clever clogs."

The next morning they were up early. Mr Balderson, wearing a frilly apron and a flamboyant air on account of a paisley bandana that he had bound at an angle across his blind eye, engaged himself, in solemn and religious silence, in the porridge. Judy started to store away the bedding and put the table back up, helped by William, who was no help at all really but she held her tongue. She was still a bit shaken by her outburst the previous night. She had thought of herself as the kind of person who didn't take out their own troubles on complete innocents, but she had been wrong. She wasn't any better than Josh and Tyler – bullies, who just hit out when it suited them. Basically, she was a nasty person. But she would start treating William as a human being, not just a pain in the neck.

When they had eaten breakfast and cleared up, they left the site and drove on across the flat expanses of Northern Germany and into Denmark, gaping at the vast windfarms and the bridges that swept in majestic curves over grey and white-flecked sounds between the islands. Judy took the opportunity to quiz Mr Balderson on the people they'd seen back at the campsite.

"Did you know those people?" she said. As expected, Mr Balderson was cryptic.

"Yes and no."

"Meaning?"

"I know them, but I don't know their names. Well, I do now, we introduced ourselves, but I didn't when we arrived. You know them too."

"No I don't."

"You, of all people, know them. You said as much to William last night."

Judy flushed. He had heard, then.

"They are 'them' to everybody with a job and a home and a car in the drive. They aren't Joe or Charlie or Mrs Green down the road, they are just 'them' – the stateless, the homeless, the unbound – and now we are them too, we belong now to the non-belonging. We have upped anchor and sailed away. This is freedom, and I've heard it said that it's not all it's cracked up to be."

Judy sat up in surprise. Those were her father's words.

"What did you say?"

"I said freedom is not all it's cracked up to be," Mr Balderson repeated. "Not everybody's cup of tea. An acquired taste. Personally, I find it suits very nicely."

Judy came to the point.

"I heard a word. You were talking, and I heard the name of a place; it was where my father comes from."

"Was it indeed?"

"Yes, and that man spoke to me in Farsi. What were you talking about?"

"Oh, this and that. There is always something interesting about lives such as theirs."

"But—"

"The thing about eavesdropping, in my humble

opinion, is that it can be fun at the time, but you must be prepared to take the consequences."

With that, Mr Balderson leant forward to twiddle the tuner of his ancient radio and find some music, leaving Judy not really sure how to respond.

8

On either side of the road, the forest marched past endlessly. The trunks of the pines were dark columns, the branches of the firs, burdened with snow, glittered in the headlights. Midnight had come and gone.

It hadn't been hard to find out where they needed to go. They had stopped at the tourist office in Helsingborg, and a smiling lady had pointed on a map to the town whose postcode Judy remembered. But getting there was another matter. Judy had looked at the map plenty of times before, but it was still a bit of a shock to realize how very long Sweden was, and that they would have to drive almost up to the Arctic Circle to get there. They had been on the road for two full days. Hour by hour the air became colder, the snow deeper, the sun lower in the sky. When, on the third day, they were at last getting closer to their destination, they decided to shorten their journey a bit by cutting across country on a side road.

As it turned out, this wasn't the best idea. The road was narrow and, although it was ploughed, the surface was compacted snow with no trace of grit to be seen.

A crystalline shower of tiny flakes had been falling for some time, whipped around by a mean, cutting wind that swirled and eddied among the trees. Now and then the wind dislodged great lumps of snow from the firs and they fell with a powdery thump into the drifts. Sometimes there was a break in the sea of trees as they passed a little piece of pasture or a patch of clear-felled land, and there the wind took hold and whipped a stream of snow-smoke off the drifts and across the road in front of them. It was like driving into a sudden milky fog – they could only see a few metres ahead.

It was very late, but as Mr Balderson pointed

out, there was nowhere they could get off the road, even if they had wanted to, and they had to try to reach civilization.

"It can't be far to the next village. There might even be a guesthouse, a wayside inn, a hostel, who knows?" he remarked cheerfully, peering through the windscreen at the snow-swept road ahead.

In the cab of the camper the heater was going full blast, but even so it was only bearably warm; Judy had her feet on the seat and her arms round her knees. Mr Balderson was wearing a strange collection of woollens, including a red-and-white striped woolly hat with ear flaps. William was sitting on the engine cowling, so he was warmest, but he had no proper backrest, and his head kept lolling forward as he drifted into sleep. Judy reached behind her and got hold of a cushion, putting it on her knees and pulling William over so that his head was in her lap.

Mr Balderson drove slowly. The road surface sparkled. The new fall had laid down a few centimetres of light powder that covered any tire tracks that may have been there before.

"We'd have been better off with winter tires, of course," said Mr Balderson conversationally, "But we'll just exercise our skills instead. Not too slow, that's the thing."

"Don't you mean not too fast?"

"No, Judy, I mean not too slow. If we get into a wheelspin on a hill we'll never get up it."

Judy bit her lip. Of course: a three-ton vehicle on an uphill gradient with practically no friction between wheels and road would be entirely dependent on forward momentum. Increasing the engine revolutions would only make things worse – that was no way to apply the work of the engine to the road. Basically, once they stopped, they'd never get started again.

"I wasn't thinking," she said.

"Good, you do far too much of that anyway," came the reply.

And that's how they carried on: not too slow, but not too fast either. At least when they were going downhill. Every time Mr Balderson touched the brakes they could feel the rear end of the camper twitch and waggle, ready to put them into a full skid and slew them helplessly sideways across the road. When, inevitably, that did happen, it wasn't really Mr Balderson's fault. They were going carefully downhill when the snowbank at the roadside ahead seemed to erupt and a huge shape broke free and leapt out in front of them. They had time to see the heavy dark brown body perched on top of absurdly long legs, and the long mournful face with a wisp of beard under its chin turn towards them, momentarily transfixed by the headlights. But a full-frontal collision with a five-hundred-kilo elk, whose massive body is at the level of the windscreen, would have meant death for everybody, not just the elk, so Mr Balderson had to brake. The rear wheels whipped round and spun the camper like a fairground ride, making them hit the snowbank side-on with a crunching *thud* while the near-side wheels slid over the invisible edge of the ditch and the elk loped off with a gangly rubbery stride and disappeared on the other side.

Judy could hardly breathe, and not just from the shock: William was on top of her and Mr Balderson was on top of William. Slowly the camper leaned over and came to a peaceful rest, nestling deep into the loose snow.

It was very quiet. They struggled to untangle themselves.

"Where are we?" asked William

"In the ditch," replied Mr Balderson.

"Can we drive out again?"

"On the whole I would say no, but I'll see if he'll start."

This wasn't easy with the camper listing like a ship on a reef. The engine turned over a couple of times, coughed and cleared its throat, but there was nothing more than that.

"We are going to need some help," said Mr Balderson. "Everybody needs help sometimes."

"But who's going to help us?" said Judy. "We haven't seen anyone for hours."

Mr Balderson looked past the edge of the ditch. "True. But the road is ploughed, so it is in use. We shall stick it out, sing songs, tell stories, and dream of things past and things to come. Could you see if the gas heater still works, Judy?"

It was dark in the camper as Judy scrambled

back through the mess. Cupboard doors had sprung open, books and jars of jam and bits of clothing and tools were everywhere. She tried to start the heater, but nothing happened.

"Temperamental at the best of times," said Mr Balderson. "There's probably snow packed in there."

Something in his voice sounded different. It was only a *little* different – a tiny bit less full of the joys and excitement of just being alive – but Judy noticed it. William shivered. He was starting to feel cold.

"Right," said Mr Balderson, "let's get organized. Get into your sleeping bags and lie close together."

"Why?" asked William.

"Because it is going to get cold," Mr Balderson replied.

"It's cold *now*."

Mr Balderson sighed. "You won't think this is cold in an hour or two, I can assure you."

It was a bothersome fussy business, in the darkness of the crazily leaning camper, to fumble around finding seat cushions and blankets and work out how to make some kind of bed. In the end, Judy and William didn't so much lie down on the couch as roll into it, with William on the inside.

"Help, Judy's squashing me, I'm squashed!"

"Good," said Mr Balderson. "The squasheder the better."

They had burrowed down as far as possible under quilts and blankets – and the clothes Mr Balderson had heaped on top of them – and Judy had made William get into her sleeping bag. Now he struggled a bit and stuck out his head.

"If someone comes past, how will we stop them?" he asked Mr Balderson.

"They'll stop. They know what's at stake here."

"And what *is* at stake?" asked Judy, though she knew really.

"Keep your head covered, Judy, and stop asking questions."

Mr Balderson was clambering around, stepping over them from time to time, rooting about and humming to himself. Quite suddenly a pale light flooded the camper. The moon had broken free from the treetops and rode low in the sky.

"Ah … as I feared, it's cleared up," said Mr Balderson. He had assembled a very mixed collection of garments for himself. To Judy, peering out from the cocoon she had made, he seemed to be about twice his normal size, as though someone had inflated him with a bike pump. He was wearing his woolly hat, but on top of it was a tea towel that he had tied under his chin. He must have been wearing at least three jumpers as well as a moth-eaten windcheater. He could hardly move his arms. Under two voluminous skirts was a pair of dirty jeans that Judy had seen stuffed into one of the bench lockers to stop a bunch of spanners from rattling about, and on his hands were at least two pairs of woollen socks.

"We should have brought some proper clothing, but there wasn't really time for that," he remarked.

"Now, in view of the weather I think I shall just walk back up the road for a bit. I'm sure we passed a farm a little way back…" He clambered awkwardly towards the door and managed with difficulty to get it open. He tumbled out.

"Time to snuggle, people. Snuggling's what does it." Then he let the door slam shut, and he was gone.

Neither William nor Judy were the kind of people who snuggled if they could possibly help it

– which just goes to show what a bit of extremely cold weather can do, because now they snuggled as though their lives depended on it. Which in fact, although neither of them mentioned it, they did.

Within half an hour the final vestiges of warmth had been sucked inexorably out of the camper as the cold seeped in. Outside, the last wisps of cloud scattered before the dying wind, and the moon rose higher in a perfectly clear sky. The temperature had dropped like a stone and there was absolute silence, the silence that only a deep midwinter night can bring: no rustlings on the forest floor, no soft twittering from birds in the branches, no fox's bark, no squirrel hastily scrabbling up a tree trunk. And so the cold – the vicious, stealthy, merciless, cracking cold – had made its dramatic entrance, stalking forest and field, poking into every crack and cranny and root and hollow tree, searching with icy fingers for small fluttering hearts to pull the life from.

In the camper, Judy had rolled herself up in the quilt and left only a little hole for her nose and mouth. The warm air that she exhaled had formed a ring of ice crystals round its edge. She looked at the condensation that had frozen instantly into a pattern on the windows of the camper, a filigree of frost.

William's muffled voice from somewhere almost underneath her said,

"My feet are cold."

"Waggle them."

"I can't, you're lying on them."

Judy moved a bit.

"Can you waggle them now?"

"Sort of."

Judy remembered playing outdoors once, in some kind of courtyard. It was one of those memories that's from so long ago that it seems like a dream. She must have been very small. But she remembered harsh sunlight, and complaining that it was too hot, and asking why it didn't get cooler.

"I shall never complain about the heat again," she said out loud.

9

The big tiled stove in the living room was almost too hot to touch. Stefan checked to see that the fire had died down properly and then reached up to close the damper. Now the heat would last all night, but he would have to get up early anyway, to light the kitchen stove and fill the wood box. He started to get ready for bed. His little room was tucked in behind the kitchen, with the chimney making part of one wall, so he was cosy enough. As he slid down under his duvet he smiled contentedly. If it was under minus thirty in the morning, he wouldn't have to go to school – and it looked like being a lot colder than that. That was the rule for pupils who came in from the outlying villages. So he could spend tomorrow with his little Ferguson, which meant he had a decision to make: renovate the DC generator and keep to his plan of restoring the whole tractor to mint condition, or weld new brackets, mount an AC generator and stop the battery losing power on him all the time. In the company of happy thoughts of condensers and distributors, Stefan fell asleep.

In the camper, William's teeth chattered.

"I can't feel my feet at all. I waggled them but it didn't help."

Judy knew that he was shivering badly.

"We'll have to change places," she said. "We need to be like penguins, William. They stand in a huddle and the ones on the outside move into the middle to get warm." Judy managed to pull and push and roll William over her so that he lay on her other side. She quickly realized why he had felt so frozen. The side of the camper was icy cold.

"W-w-what if nobody comes?" William wanted to know.

"Oh, we'll be all right," Judy said breezily.

To her relief, William seemed satisfied with this. It was the kind of thing an air hostess would say if the engines conked out at thirty thousand feet, she thought grimly. On the other hand, what else was there to say? The outlook seemed fairly poor to her, but there wasn't any point discussing it with William. In fact, she guessed there was a clear possibility of them actually dying, not just being frozen and uncomfortable and miserable. For a brief moment, she tried out of sheer habit to calculate the probability of survival, but she just didn't have enough information about this kind of thing to even make a decent stab at it. Forty per cent? Fifty? One and a half? She felt drowsy. But, no, she mustn't go to sleep. She knew that much.

"Do you think Mr Balderson will be back soon?" William wondered.

"Yes, he won't be long."

She didn't know how long Mr Balderson could last outside, even if he kept moving. She had a feeling that it wasn't very long. Twenty minutes? Half an hour? But this was all just guesswork, and she didn't like guesswork.

"We could make a grèat big bonfire and get really warm," said William's voice in her ear. "There are about a million trees, would anybody mind?"

"I don't think they'd mind much, but I don't think we could actually do it. Four feet of snow, no proper clothing, one little axe. It's pretty hard to make a fire even when it's not cold and snowy. I'm not much good at camp fires at the best of times."

"And I've never done it before."

"Well there you are then. We'd be all at sea."

William's head emerged from his sleeping bag.

"If it *was* the sea then this would be a boat, but it's not. And we would be shipwrecked, not crashed, and send up a flare."

"That's a good thought, William, but I'm pretty sure we don't have any flares."

Suddenly Judy's head had pictures in it that started turning into an idea. If it didn't work, they would definitely be done for…

"But it should work," she said to herself. *Think, Judy.* How many things could go wrong? She got to eight things that definitely could go wrong, and gave up counting.

Judy emerged from her nest, and tucked her quilt and blankets around William.

"W-where are you going?"

"You gave me an idea, William. You're a genius."

"Am I?"

"Well no, but at least it was an idea."

Judy climbed forward, took the keys out of the ignition and pushed open the door on the driver's side. She half scrambled, half rolled out into the moonlit road, brushing snow that was as dry as desert sand from her clothes. Every drop of moisture was frozen out of the world. She had thought that inside the camper was as cold as it could possibly be, but she was wrong. Out here, she couldn't breathe through her nose; her nostrils stuck together when she inhaled. She breathed carefully through half-open lips. She had a small key to open the hatch that was set into the side of the camper, but her hands were horribly fumbly and the two pairs of woollen socks on her hands weren't helping much. In about five minutes her hands wouldn't work at all. If it had been a game at a children's party, or one of those idiotic TV programmes where the contestants make fools of themselves, then it would have been funny. It wasn't funny now.

She lifted each of her feet in turn, up and down, up and down, as she tried to delay the moment they would turn into blocks of ice. Finally she got the key into the keyhole, but it wouldn't turn. The lock was frozen.

Now at last she felt real fear. She didn't want to die. She wanted to be back in England, where being cold meant an extra jumper and a cup of tea; not here, where the cold was a force of nature as deadly as a tidal wave or a hurricane or an erupting volcano. She was an alien here, a living creature, a bag made of skin and filled with blood and muscle and bone, flowing and bubbling and burping and digesting and totally at odds with the dry, lifeless, crystalline beautiful desert that is a winter landscape at under minus forty degrees. Tears of sheer frustration froze into little pearls on Judy's eyelashes, and her eyelids started sticking together. She blinked and rubbed at them.

Heat it, said a clear calm voice, right in the middle of her head. *Heat the key*.

Judy groped in her pocket with her socked hand and took out the lighter.

She clicked it. Nothing. But the second time it lit, and Judy held the key over the weak yellow flame and saw it blacken. She pushed it into the lock and forced herself to count to five. It was enough. The key turned and she opened the hatch. Inside were two propane cylinders. She rolled them out into the road.

"Minimum fifty metres. But that's another guess," she mumbled.

Still in the desperate hurry that the body, with no help from the mind, seems to generate all by itself in such a cold, she dragged the cylinders down the road. The chill of the metal handles made it feel like they were slicing through the socks on her hands like a scalpel. Propping them up beside each other in the snow at the roadside, one slightly higher than the other, she opened the valve of the lower one, directing it on to its neighbour. At once the propane hissed out. Not too much at first, she said to herself. Judy clicked the lighter, and kept on clicking and clicking. At last it worked, and she lit the gas before opening the valve completely so that the blue flame could roar straight on to the other cylinder. There was no time to watch. With a slow turn, Judy half-jogged back to the camper; if she moved any faster then the slight wind her speed created was unbearable. Scrambling back into the camper she buried herself, shaking and shivering, in the pile of cushions and blankets and sleeping bags and old clothes that had William in it somewhere.

How long could it last, the propane flame, going full blast? Would it heat the other cylinder enough? And if it did work, were they far enough away? How hot could it get, when the heat was constantly sucked out of it by the freezing air? She should have covered the cylinders with something – a blanket, anything – but they couldn't spare them and there hadn't been time. Maybe a bag would have done it? Her holdall. But there hadn't been time; she would have frozen to death. Judy felt frozen now. Going outside had pushed her to the point where she felt she would never be warm again. She had brought the cold in with her – in her hands and feet and blood.

"William. William?"

She started worrying at William like a puppy with a favourite toy. "Don't go to sleep, rub your hands together, wiggle your toes."

William didn't answer.

She felt for his body in the pile, drew him towards her and wrapped her arms around him. Then she waited.

A sudden flash, like lightning, illuminated the camper, to be followed a millisecond later by a deafening explosion that sounded horribly close. Something bounced off the roof.

Stefan sat up in bed. Something had woken him up. He listened but there was nothing. Sometimes when the cold came suddenly the trunk of a birch tree split open with a crack like a pistol shot, when the last sap of autumn froze and swelled. But not now, surely? And anyway, it wouldn't have woken him up like that. His bedroom door opened slowly, and in the moonlight he saw his grandmother with a shawl over her shoulders.

"Stefan, did you hear? Something's happened, down the road a way. A big bang."

"Yes. It woke me up."

"It's not right. You must go and see what it is."

"Nobody's out tonight. I'll go in the morning and look then if you like."

"Please go now. It was a boom, like the war. Perhaps an invasion has started."

"I don't think the Russians will come tonight."

Stefan's grandmother was mostly perfectly sensible and calm. But what happens to a young child is there for ever, and she was only six years old when the Russians invaded Finland, the country of her birth.

"Stefan…"

He was already out of bed and pulling his trousers on. "I'm on my way."

He went out into the hall and continued dressing. Thick woollen socks, woollen jumper, winter overall, a parka with a fur-lined hood, heavy lined boots and his mittens. It should be enough to keep out the cold. He opened the inner front door, and closed it behind him as he opened the outer door before walking across the yard to the shed where the tractor stood ready. Stefan climbed up into the cab and started the engine, lifting the snow-blade attached to the rear. He turned the heater on full, leaving the fan for a bit to give it time to warm up. It was a cold night.

As he drove out of the shed and down the track towards the road, he looked around. The night was as beautiful as a winter night can be. The birches cast a tangled calligraphy of moon-shadows across the white meadows, each branch a pen-stroke precisely marked. Every half-buried fence post wore a hat of snow, like a line of chefs at a royal banquet. With the moon almost full, only the strongest stars were visible, and a planet or two. He could have driven without headlights and still seen perfectly clearly.

As he rounded the first bend with the snow-chains rattling and clinking on the frozen surface, he saw a large black hole in the snow at the roadside. Just beyond it there was a van of some kind in the ditch. It didn't belong to anybody he knew, and he knew *everybody* around here.

Stefan stopped beside the van – some kind of motor caravan that was almost an antique. It had wedged itself fairly thoroughly into the ditch. But there were no big boulders just here, so whoever had been driving was lucky. He looked at the front wheel hanging forlornly in the air. No one in their right mind would drive on these roads on those tires. They must be Stockholmers, or most likely foreigners. He brushed snow from the front. It was a UK number plate, as far as he could tell.

He heard someone scraping away the frost from the window of the cab, and made out a pale face behind the glass, wrapped in a motley assortment of what seemed to be rags. The door opened. He would have to test his English.

"Hello, my name is Stefan," he said. That seemed to have gone well, because the person started talking a lot, very fast through chattering teeth. He didn't get much of it. But he got "help" and he could figure out the rest.

"Come out," said Stefan. "Go in there." He pointed to the tractor. When the person got out, Stefan could see that it was probably a girl. But she didn't climb into the tractor, just stood there shaking and gesticulating towards the camper. Then she climbed back in. Stefan got the point. He climbed in after her and saw her rooting around in a pile of blankets and cushions, exposing a sleeping bag with somebody in it. Together they got the person out of the camper. "His name's William," said Judy, as Stefan put him over his shoulder, took a step up into the tractor cab and placed him in the space behind the seat as gently as he could. How long had these people been here? This one wasn't moving, and Stefan couldn't even tell if he was breathing. Stefan stepped back down and looked at the girl. Incredibly, she was wearing trainers with tea towels wrapped round them, socks on her hands and jeans, together with an odd collection of scarves and jumpers. Who had been driving? She didn't look old enough. But he would have to find out the answers to his questions later.

"We must go. It is cold for your feet tonight."

Sheer relief had made Judy light-headed. "Really?" she said. "You don't say?"

"But I do say this. It is not good for your toes."

That joke fell flat, thought Judy, as she moved towards the cab.

"No," said Stefan. "First me."

Stefan climbed up and for a terrifying moment

Judy thought that he had changed his mind and decided to leave her there. So much for witty remarks. But he leaned down towards her.

"Now you."

"Where? There's no room."

"On me. Sit on me."

This was not at all what Judy wanted, but she could see there was no choice. The cold had seeped ever deeper into hands and feet and face, and now she could hardly move. She tried to get a foot on to the step, but she couldn't lift it. Her body was shutting down. Before she could try again, a mittened hand reached down and took hold of her arm, yanking her into the cab.

Stefan sat her in his lap. She wasn't very big, and if she sat sideways he could get at the pedals and the steering wheel. He managed to slam the door, and immediately the roaring heater fan took hold of the air in the cab. As the warmth struck her face, Judy gave up caring that she was sitting in the lap of a total stranger, trapped between his arms. They were alive, and, blissfully, there was warmth. The bliss didn't last very long. As the warm air penetrated her trainers, pain stabbed her feet. She gasped.

"Now your toes have hurt, I think," said a voice in her ear.

"Yes."

"Good."

"Good?"

"Yes, good. They are still alive."

Stefan was pretty happy with himself. He'd had a conversation in English, and that would please his grandmother, who was always worrying that he wasn't working hard enough in his English classes at school. Which was perfectly true.

10

The tractor rattled up the track towards Stefan's home, and in the moonlight Judy saw a single-storey timbered farmhouse with outhouses on either side. The yard was ploughed clear of drifts, but around the walls the snow reached almost to the window sills, and the roofs looked as though huge white duvets had been thrown over them. They glinted and glittered in the moonlight. It was a fairy-tale sight – warm welcoming light in the windows, a lamp lit above the covered porch where fir branches had been spread to clear boot-soles of snow before you entered the house. The outhouses were much bigger than the house itself. To the left a huge timbered barn rose on great granite posts, and to the right there was a long, low building. The tractor came to a halt right outside the front door and Stefan reached over and swung the cab door open.

"Please, in the house."

Judy scrambled awkwardly down, followed by Stefan who helped manhandle an inert William out. They carried him between them towards the door, and Judy opened it to find another door facing her. As she reached for the handle the door swung inwards to reveal the shy face of an elderly woman who smiled at them and beckoned them in, saying something in Swedish and shaking her head a little. Stefan replied.

"Oh, you are English," the woman said. "Then you have come a long way. Please, come in and go into the kitchen, it is warmest there." Her voice had a Scandinavian lilt to it, but she spoke English almost perfectly. Stefan said a few words to the woman, who turned to Judy.

"Who was driving you?"

"Mr Balderson; he went back up the road to get help."

There was more fast Swedish, and then Stefan

was on his way out again.

"Farmor speaks English very good, " he said over his shoulder.

"Farmer?" said Judy after a moment of puzzled silence. She was feeling more confused by the minute. The woman laughed. "It means grandmother, not farmer. Father's mother – far, mor. After the war – the Winter War, you know – I was in England for almost three years. But I'm afraid I have lost some words. I can read books, of course, but in conversation—"

William stirred, bringing their attention back to him. He was pale and still shivering when they pulled him out of his sleeping bag, but he managed to stand so Farmor could herd them into the kitchen.

The room they entered was big – the whole width of the house. The ceiling was low, made even lower by wooden beams, and the scrubbed pine floorboards were wide, covered here and there by long woven rugs. There was a long wooden table, with a settle on one side against the wall, and chairs on the other sides. But the big black stove with its huge hob was what they were drawn to, as though it was a big black magnet.

"That's right," said Farmor, drawing chairs up to the stove. She took a couple of logs out of the wood box and poked them into the firebox. Judy and William sat as close as they could, stretching out their hands in that age-old open-handed gesture that felt as natural as breathing. The heat flowed towards them. Meanwhile Farmor was bustling about. She put on a kettle, took down cups from the dresser. As she moved around the kitchen she spoke.

"Stefan will look for your friend. Was he dressed like you are dressed?"

She spoke kindly, but in spite of Judy's exhaustion she could hear the anxiety in Farmor's voice.

"Yes, you could say that."

"Oh. How long has he been gone?"

Judy had to think about that.

"About an hour. Hour and a half. Maybe more. I'm not really sure."

Farmor said no more. At the sink she filled a zinc bucket with warm water and from a cupboard she took a tin, spooning out a yellow powder that she carefully stirred into the water. She lifted the bucket, and brought it to the stove.

"Perhaps he should be first," she said, and she pulled William's chair back so that she could kneel down in front of him. "I'm called Sara Petterson."

"I'm William Parkinson."

He watched as she removed his shoes and socks and shook her head at his feet, which were a pale whitish blue and still cold to the touch.

She drew the bucket closer.

"What are you doing?" said William.

"A mustard bath for your feet. It is the best way, but the water must reach up to your calves. You must take off your trousers, they are too tight to roll up properly."

"No."

"But really, it is true, and you will be warm again soon."

"No."

Judy had been on her way to a deep sleep, on the verge of falling off her chair, but she sensed rather than saw William beginning to tense up. She roused herself and saw his head go back, and his eyes start to slip upwards.

"I don't think he can do it, Mrs Petterson. He can't always... New things, and people..." She broke off. You couldn't really explain William, you just had to hope that people would understand.

"Of course," said Farmor. "It is difficult. Perhaps Stefan?"

"Well, I wouldn't be too sure," said Judy.

On cue, the kitchen door opened and Stefan came in. Farmor looked up quickly, and Judy saw Stefan give a quick shake of the head. Without all his outdoor gear on Judy could see that he really was just a boy, probably a bit older than her but not that much. She hadn't expected that, what with all that gruff ordering them about and the way he had driven the tractor and got them out of the mess. He had light brown, almost blond hair, blue eyes, a blob of a nose and freckles which were about as boyish as you could get. But his wide shoulders said something else, and his hands were a working man's hands, with broad palms and long fingers.

Farmor started talking to Stefan in rapid Swedish.

He walked over to William.

"Hello, my name is Stefan."

"I'm William Parkinson."

"I is living here. Is I speaking good English?"

"No. It's 'am I?', not 'is I?'"

"Oh, am it?" Stefan frowned, but he was enjoying himself. His English was bad, but it wasn't that bad.

"No," said William. "*Is it*. You must say 'is it.'"

"I think you must help me. Is you cold?"

"Are you cold," said William, getting a bit impatient. "Yes I AM."

"Me too, we will go and get warm and learn English. Come."

William stood up, but he didn't look as if he was going anywhere on his frozen feet. Before he could protest, Stefan had hoisted him on to his broad back and walked out of the door, with William riding piggyback and either too surprised or simply too cold and exhausted to do anything about it.

The ache in Judy's toes had given way to a sort of tingling itch. She heard the front door slam, and looking out of the window she saw the figure of Stefan stamping across the moonlit farmyard with

William on his back bouncing up and down like a sack of potatoes.

"He's taking him outside again! He'll die!"

"No, no, please don't worry. He must get warm properly, as soon as possible. Or he might become ill. Please trust me. We have been cold before, you understand."

Judy felt a bit embarrassed. Of *course* they knew what they were doing. This was their habitat, not hers. They lived their lives here. And they had just saved her life, with no fuss at all, as though it was the sort of thing you do every day.

"I'm sorry," said Judy, "and thank you. Thank you so much for saving us."

"I hope you'll be all right on the sofa in the living room?" Farmor asked kindly. "Come along and I'll show you. Just put your things outside the door."

She intended to let Judy's clothes spend the night outdoors in the yard. That would kill anything that was creeping around in there. They must have been on the road for quite some time, and she couldn't be too sure what state they had been in to start with.

Farmor led Judy down the hall to the living room. It wasn't big, but the word cosy could have been invented for it. The timbered walls were covered with faded hand-painted wallpaper in a floral pattern. There was a proper stuffed sofa, a leather chair, with a standard lamp next to it, a shelf of books, and in one corner an old grandfather clock painted blue, with a design of flowers on the panels. In the opposite corner a big round tiled stove reached up to the ceiling, topped with a crown of white tiles and, low down, about a foot from the floor, brass doors for the firebox. It spread its delicious warmth through the room. On the sofa was a huge feather duvet, and a pillow. Judy looked at it and wondered if she had the willpower to even remove a scrap of clothing. Still, she made herself shed most of her jumpers and jeans, and put them outside the door in a heap before crawling under the duvet.

"Oh thank you, thank you, thank you," she said, this time to the stove, and the duvet, and the pillow. She wondered what had happened to William and worried about Mr Balderson, but then she was gone, tumbling down into a deep well of sleep.

The little wood-panelled room Stefan and William had entered had a low bench on one side, and hooks along the wall. Stefan sat the boy down on the bench and stuck his head into the sauna. It was still pretty warm; there was a bed of live coals in the firebox. He stuffed in as much wood as it would take, and heard the logs crackle and catch with a woof that soon settled into a low, satisfying roar. Then he went back and undressed. He bent over William, and tried to start drawing his pullover over his head. But William leaned over on the bench, curled his legs up under him, and clutched at his clothes. Stefan felt his hands. They were icy, and the more he tensed the colder he got.

Stefan spoke as he would have spoken to his little cousin Maria.

"It is time for the bath."

"I don't want to have a bath."

"When did you have a bath last time?"

"I can't remember."

"Was it a lot of days since then?"

"Yes."

"Then you are dirty. Take off your clothes."

"I don't want to."

"Do you in England have a bath in your clothes?"

"…No."

"Not in Sweden either. Do like me."

William opened one eye and squinted up at the boy standing naked in front of him. Slowly he sat up and started fumbling at his pullover. Stefan helped him, and before too long he was ensconced on the lowest tier in the sauna, where the heat wouldn't knock him out. Stefan sat higher up and looked at William's back. *No wonder he was cold*, he thought, *he's so skinny I can count his vertebrae*.

Slowly William came back to life. He wasn't used to being completely naked in company – it's not something that happens very often in England, at least not with people whom you don't know very well. But the boy who was sitting there on the bench above him seemed to think it was perfectly normal. And it wouldn't have been a good idea to have clothes on, because it really was very hot.

"I'm too hot. I have to go out."

"Not yet, you are still dry."

"But I can hardly breathe. My nose hurts."

"Your mouth, you must use your mouth."

William breathed through his mouth and it was a bit better, but he still felt as though he might burst into flames at any moment. It was very odd that the bits of him that were usually warmest, like under his armpits, were now the bits that were cold. Suddenly he realized that his find, which had been hanging around his neck on a piece of string, was gone. He looked around, started to get up. Had it fallen off? When?

"It is outside. I took it off. You cannot have metal on you, it will burn you. Please sit down, soon it will be time."

William didn't really mind just doing as he was told. He wasn't afraid of the boy at all – he wasn't a bit like Josh and Tyler. Josh and Tyler smiled and sniggered and that always meant trouble. This boy never smiled, but his eyes looked at William as though he was working out what was best for him, not what was worst. Still, the heat was getting to be unbearable. William felt his scalp tickle, and quite suddenly sweat started to trickle down his forehead and behind his ears. It dropped from the end of his nose, and ran down his back in streams. He was practically soaked.

"*Now* we go out."

Thankful, William got up and opened the door to the sauna, going straight to the pegs where his clothes hung. His find was hanging on its string on a peg of its own.

"Wait," said Stefan.

He was carrying a wooden bucket and he opened the outer door, walking straight out into the night. In a few seconds he was back. The bucket was full of snow. He scooped out a handful and advanced on William.

William backed up against the wall. This boy was going to attack him, just like Josh and Tyler. Perhaps Swedish bullies were different from English ones, and that was why he had been fooled.

"Leave me alone!"

Stefan had instantly seen William turn from a tired boy into a hunted animal, and he was furious with himself for being so stupid. Someone like

William, it was obvious.

So Stefan took the handful of snow and plonked it down on his own head, saying, "Oof, oy-oy-oy." Then he took another handful and started rubbing it over the rest of him, hopping around and shouting "Aaah, what a nice bath!"

William laughed. Then Stefan took a towel and dried himself off.

"Now it is your turn. Can you do it?"

William did it. The snow was like an electric shock, but as he rubbed it all over himself he felt the warmth lock into his body.

"You close your skin, you shut the door. Inside you stay hot," said Stefan.

It was true. William dried himself and put his clothes on, and as they walked back to the house through the frozen night that had come close to killing him, it felt as though it was a pleasant spring evening.

Farmor smiled and nodded when William came back into the house pink-cheeked. She put a finger to her lips and beckoned so that he followed her through the kitchen. On the floor of Stefan's room was a mattress, a duvet and a pillow. William lay down, pulled the duvet up to his chin, and with his hand on his chest clutching his find, he fell asleep.

11

Judy woke up and lay for a while under the warm duvet wondering where she was and how she had got there. The room was still dark, darker than before in fact, for the moon had set. But the sky was now a sombre purply-red. It was daybreak, so she couldn't have slept very long; they had been so late getting to bed. But she felt rested. She got up and switched on the lamp that stood beside the sofa, seeing a neat pile of clothes on the armchair. Not hers. There was a checked shirt, sort of lumberjack-style, and a pair of baggy green trousers. It wasn't the kind of stuff she would have chosen to wear, but she got dressed and combed her fingers through her hair in the hope that the result was acceptable. Sort of tousled was all right, but not dragged-through-the-hedge-backwards. She was thirsty. She made her way quietly to the kitchen and opened the door. To her surprise, it was warm and lit and the table already held the remains of breakfast. But now only William was still sitting there, eating a thick piece of bread and butter. Farmor was removing a big coffee pot from the stove. A silver-grey dog with friendly brown eyes left its place by the stove and came over to say hello, but returned and lay down again on a sharp word from Farmor.

"Silla should be outside," she said, "but I am glad of the company these days. And like me, she is not as young as she used to be. Good morning," she went on, "We have some news. They have found him – your friend. Sven saw something sticking out of a snowdrift. The top of a red woollen hat."

"Is he...?" Judy couldn't help imagining the deep-frozen lump that their odd travelling companion must have become.

"He is alive…" Farmor hesitated. "Or he seems to be. It is very strange. They were sure he was gone – he should not be alive, it should be impossible.

They were taking him away in the ambulance, and they found that his heart was beating. Very very slowly, like a bear in the winter. He may survive. Sven told me this morning..." Judy looked at the clock on the wall above the settle. It was half past ten. No wonder she felt rested.

"Good. That's good. But where will they take him?"

"His case is so interesting and unusual that they will fly him down to Uppsala, I should think. We will hear if they think he will live. Try not to worry."

Judy wasn't worried. She thought that Mr Balderson would be very hard indeed to kill.

Farmor sat her down at the table and made sure that everything was within reach – bread and sour milk and jam and honey and muesli. Then she poured coffee into a mug.

"Or perhaps you would like tea?" she asked. One of the things Farmor remembered most clearly about her stay in England was that everybody drank gallons and gallons of tea at every possible opportunity, and that what they called coffee tasted like old dishwater. Judy said that coffee was fine. Looking at the food she realized that she was ravenously hungry. In the quiet, it occurred to Judy that one of the really positive things about William was that if he didn't have anything he wanted to say, he didn't speak. No "How did you sleep?" or "I wonder what the weather will be like today?" No small talk. At breakfast this is a very fine quality, Judy thought. Being nice and polite and making conversation is all very well, but if you can avoid it during breakfast, that is even better. Farmor was also quietly busy at the sink, and slowly the light changed until a single pale ray of sun found its way through the window and made a bright spot on the wall beside the clock.

"He will be back soon, I'm sure."

"Who? Back from where?"

"Stefan. He went out to get your van."

"Oh." Judy had vaguely imagined that he was still in bed somewhere.

"We will see what Stefan can do. He is very good with machines. Young, but he is soon the best in the village."

"He mustn't go to too much trouble. Perhaps he could tow it to a garage or something?"

"A very long way. And he loves to do it. It is his best thing, much better than schoolwork. Even better than fishing, and anyway there is too much snow on the ice for fishing. Now, if you are finished, we will find some warm clothes for you. Then you can go outside and get some fresh air. Perhaps you could go down to the mailbox and see if they have managed to get the newspaper delivered today. It is not too cold. I think you found the hardest night of the year. Now it will change."

After breakfast they went out into the hall and Farmor kitted them out. She had made a huge heap of clothes on the hall floor – everything from hats and scarves to boots – and they rifled through. Judy's feet were about the same size as Farmor's, so she got a really nice pair of leather boots with funny pointed-up toes like the prow of a boat. William's feet were positively huge for someone his age, and a pair of Stefan's boots did well enough. There were down jackets and fleeces and lined overalls, and a vast array of hats, from proper fur-lined ones with earflaps to knitted woollen caps with bobbles and even a tassel or two. William stood there mostly while they tested various bits of clothing on him, only protesting when they tried to touch his head. He picked out a red woollen hat with a long pointy top that was more like a windsock than a hat. Judy said that it made him look like a garden gnome, but this just made him cheerful, and he wouldn't wear anything else. It was the gnome hat or nothing.

By the time they were fully clothed they were far too hot to stay indoors, so it was a relief to step outside. Farmor's idea of "not too cold" was minus twenty-one degrees, and Judy had been expecting the worst, but with proper clothing and the light in their faces it was a world away from the trials of the night before. The sun had crept over the horizon, and its rays, almost parallel with the ground, arrowed through the pine trees that fringed the home acres, turning their trunks a rosy red. The weathered gable-end of the timbered barn was that warm deep reddish brown colour that only pitch and a couple of hundred years can create. And the snow! Every crystal of snow was a prism that flashed the colours of the rainbow as the light moved across it. In every snowdrift, in the great piles that had been heaped around the yard, in the billows of untouched snow on every roof, a million opals shone.

The snow creaked drily under their boots as they walked across the yard.

"I'm going to make a great big snowball," said William. "It snowed once at home and I rolled a big ball. But it was full of muck. This is very white and clean. You start with a little one and then you roll it."

He scooped up some snow and tried to form it in his hands, but it was impossible. The snow was a dry powder and he might as well have tried to make a ball out of a handful of dust. They left the yard and walked down the track towards the road, their eyes half-closed against the light and their breath floating away like smoke into the sky, which was now the palest of blues. The mailbox was just visible, peeking out from its little niche in the ploughed-up snow at the roadside. When they were about halfway down they heard the sound of a heavy engine and the clink of snow-chains as Stefan's tractor eased itself off the road and up towards the farm with Ari the camper in tow. Judy and William had to step off the track, standing up to their knees in snow as they were passed. Things didn't look too good for the camper. It waddled like a drunken duck, and at least one of the rear wheels wobbled so much that it looked as though it might collapse at any moment.

"Stefan will mend it," said William, with complete certainty.

Judy wasn't so sure.

When they returned with the newspaper, the camper had disappeared, swallowed up somewhere in the great barn that was the workshop, machine shed, hayloft, everything.

Later Judy and William tried to help Farmor prepare the evening meal. At first she said, "no, no, you must rest," which Judy thought meant, "please stay out of my way". But she relented in the end, when she saw that they really did want to be some kind of help. William was allowed to go out to the woodshed with an empty wood-basket. He didn't come back, but that didn't seem to bother Farmor at all. Judy was allowed to peel potatoes, with Farmor hovering anxiously until she saw how neatly

Judy worked – the result of living in a houseboat with a tiny kitchen. Eventually William did return, without the wood-basket.

"Where's the wood?" asked Judy.

"I forgot it. Look what I found. It was hanging on the wall in the shed." He held out a rusty iron object, a cruel-looking hook and spike combined.

"I think it's an old weapon. I've seen them in the museum at home."

Farmor turned from the stove where she was poking the potatoes.

"It's a timber-hook but I'm afraid it's not as old as that. It was Stefan's great-grandfather's. They used to float timber down the rivers to the sawmill on the coast. If there was a big logjam, they walked out on to it and hooked the timber free. Very dangerous work. The shaft was three metres long, but it was used for kindling long ago."

"I'll go and put it back in the shed," said William, trying not to sound too disappointed.

"If you want it, you can have it. No timber has been floated for years and years. It's all road transport now."

"Thank you very much." William's face shone. "I bet no one in England has one. I'll show it to Mr Greaves."

We won't be seeing Mr Greaves any time soon, thought Judy, but there was no point in rubbing it in. William disappeared into Stefan's room.

Farmor turned to Judy.

"What a lucky boy. He finds things, and they make him happy," she said quietly.

Judy had never thought of William as lucky before.

"I suppose so," she said doubtfully.

"And he doesn't just find things," said Farmor.

"How do you mean?"

"He found you."

It had been dark for several hours when Stefan came in at last and they all sat down to eat boiled potatoes, pickled herring and sauerkraut.

"Stefan thinks he can fix it," said Farmor. "He has lots of tools. It will take some time, but you must wait anyway, to see what happens to your Mr Balderson."

"We can find somewhere to stay. Is there a youth hostel or something in the village?"

But Farmor was having none of it. There was nowhere better to stay for miles around, and they had plenty of room.

"You can of course sleep in the living room, and William can sleep in the kitchen, in the settle. Stefan's grandfather slept in that settle as a child, and he died there too. You just lift the lid, and there you are."

Mr Balderson would have liked that, thought Judy. But William didn't.

"I want to stay in Stefan's room."

"What about asking *Stefan* if he wants someone on his floor?" said Judy.

"Do you want someone on your floor?" asked William immediately.

Stefan looked at him seriously. "Of course I do. If you will not snore."

"Judy said—"

"That's it, William," said Judy. "End of—"

"Conversation, I know."

12

Days turned into a week, and one week turned into two. The days were short, and the nights were endless. Stefan went back to school, and when he wasn't in school he was in the workshop with the camper, and William. At first Judy was worried about that. But if he hadn't wanted William there, he wouldn't have shouted, "William, now we go to work!" in a cheerful voice as soon as he had got in and had something to eat. He didn't seem to think he needed *her* out there, though. She didn't mind that. The hard thing was that it was one thing to be on the move, travelling, but it was something else to be simply stuck, sitting in someone else's house for days on end doing nothing much. Not that she was indoors all the time. Farmor lent her a pair of skis, and she was quick to pick up the smooth steady gliding stride of cross-country technique, covering miles of terrain in the tracks left by snowmobiles, or doing her own laborious pathfinding, picking her way carefully through dense forest. Once, from behind a snow-covered boulder, she thought she caught sight of a pair of tufted ears. A lynx, said Stefan. But mostly there was only the silence and the snow; sometimes the screech of a woodpecker or the raucous guffaw of a raven. Nevertheless there were many hours of darkness to fill, and a lot of them were spent in front of the tiled stove, reading and thinking.

In the parlour there was a whole shelf of English books that Farmor had collected as a young girl in England. One evening Judy picked up *Rewards and Fairies* by Kipling and opened its pages at "The Thousandth Man", remembering the envelope from Sweden that marked the poem's place in her father's book. She read the last verse lots of times,

Nine hundred and ninety-nine can't bide
The shame or mocking or laughter

But the thousandth man will stand by your side
To the gallows-foot, and after.

She didn't like that line about the gallows one little bit. But she couldn't help reading it again and again. If Rashid was in trouble, then her father would do anything to help him, even it meant getting in serious, dangerous trouble. The door opened and Farmor came in with a dustpan, although Judy couldn't see a speck of dust anywhere in the room. She stood for a moment and looked at Judy, who was lying on her back on the rug with the book beside her. Then she sat down on the sofa.

"Tell me some more about your father," said Farmor. "What is he like?"

Judy said nothing for a moment, then she sat up.

"He goes on a lot about debts – and duties and values. He says that England is a wonderful country to be in. He says that when he hears grown-ups moaning about the National Health Service, or children whining for the latest smartphone, he wants to shout at them and say that every morning they should wake up and weep for joy because they live under an English sky, with English laws and English policemen and cupcakes."

"Cupcakes?"

"He loves cupcakes. He loves England. But sometimes he says that too many people are alone in our country. That old men who have served their families all their lives are looked after by nurses, even though they have perfectly healthy kids. That some people don't even know the names of their second cousins. That the duties of family are not a burden but a gift from God. He says that when I was born, he and my mum knew they had to leave. They couldn't let me grow up there. He was so sad. When he cut himself off from his language and his people … for him it was worse than cutting off his own arm. But they told him to go, his family and his friends. They helped him, even though by then it was dangerous even to be seen with him. A friend is someone who is there even when everyone else has gone, even when your danger is their danger too. 'And I know this, Judy, because otherwise I would not be here today, and neither would you,' that's what he says."

"True friendship is sometimes hard to bear, I think," said Farmor. "Is it enough to make him leave his beloved child all alone? Is that the kind of man he is?"

"Yes," said Judy, with complete certainty.

Farmor made a sound that was somewhere between a tut and a sigh, and got up to sweep away the invisible dust. When she had gone Judy stood up and found herself pacing the room.

It was simple: she should have heard from him long ago. He had put himself in danger and he hadn't come back. She'd always imagined a happy ending to her adventure, like in a book. But not all stories have happy endings. When it came down to it, what did she have to go on? Just an address in Sweden, and now they were stranded. If she had taken that bus ride instead, hidden up somewhere in England... But no. It was just too pathetic. At least they were doing something – or would be if Mr Balderson wasn't lying in a hospital ward and the camper wasn't in microscopic pieces in Stefan's workshop. How much longer would it take to get it back on the road?

Judy went out into the hall. Boots, mittens, jacket – it was already routine for her to dress like a spacewoman every time she left the house. She stepped outside. There had been no glorious sunset today, just the pale sky shading into blue, then deeper blue as the first stars appeared, then black. Now the whole cavernous vault of the sky was spangled with stars, the constellations – Orion, Taurus, Leo – picked out to perfection, the lacy gauze of the Milky Way unfurled across it. It was amazing, to be able to see so clearly by starlight. Judy gazed upward, turning slowly round where she stood.

"Not much in the way of twinkle, though," she said to herself.

At the horizon, a bit of twinkle maybe, but in the zenith the air was too crystal clear for that – the stars shone hard and bright. Nothing is ever quite as you expect it to be when you're actually there. Judy had heard about the long dark winters of the far North, and they sounded pretty grim. But she hadn't heard anything about how the snow looks like a million glittering diamonds, or that the brightness of moonlight on snow means that you can stand outside and read a book in the middle of the night.

"Well, you could if it wasn't so cold," said Judy, and she headed off in the direction of the barn. She was going to visit the workshop, even though she hadn't actually been invited in.

Stefan was doing a thorough job on the camper. It wasn't something he decided. He just didn't know any other way. Luckily he had William. When William had followed him into the workshop, Stefan had been prepared to keep a careful eye on him, and perhaps reckoned on him not being able to concentrate properly on getting things done. But he had quickly discovered that William was the perfect workmate. William was an arranger, he was incapable of being bored, and he never chattered. He asked questions sometimes, but only if he wanted to know the answer, and most of what Stefan was doing didn't interest William very much. William would stand and wait while Stefan removed nuts, bolts, screws and gaskets, and handed them to him one by one. Then he took them, cleaned them with fluid or a wire brush and arranged them all in perfectly straight lines on the workbench. Nothing was ever lost, everything could be put back in the reverse order that it had been taken out. If Stefan said, "Hold this," then William held it until Stefan told him to let go. If Stefan, lying under the camper or buried up to the shoulders in the engine, asked him for a seventeen millimetre spanner, he went and got it, and when Stefan was finished with it he took it and hung it back on its peg in exactly the right place. But progress was slow. The whole package of leaf springs, rear axle, cardan – not to mention the entire rear suspension and transmission systems – was removed, taken apart, cleaned up and examined. It took Stefan a whole evening just to get the wheel bearings loose.

"How old is the van?" he'd asked Judy at supper that evening.

"Oh, about forty years, I think."

"When did they last grease the bearings?"

"I haven't the foggiest."

"I'm sorry, I don't—"

"I don't know, Stefan."

Stefan had decided to get the entire chassis into what he called "a good state". In the workshop he gave William a welder's mask and told him not to remove it on pain of instant banishment, and he got to work, grinding, welding and treating with anti-corrosion paint, sealant and all the rest of it.

When Judy stepped into the workshop, which was warmed by a huge, iron wood-burning contraption that Stefan had designed and constructed himself, she was met by what appeared to be two aliens from a sci-fi film and the crackling white light of an acetylene welding torch. As soon as Stefan caught sight of her he turned off the torch. Pushing back the mask from his face, he frowned.

"Why are you here?"

Judy bristled. "Is it private? I'm sorry."

"No. But it is dangerous if you look at the gas flame. You will injure your eyes."

Judy decided to be nice and polite. She looked around at the pieces of the camper that were spread about the floor, and all the small bits lined up neatly on the workbench.

"This is fantastic, Stefan. It will be like new again."

To William, who was standing close-by with his welding mask still covering his face, she said,

"You can take it off, William, he's stopped welding."

"Can I take it off, Stefan?"

For some reason William asking Stefan instead of doing what he was told annoyed Judy very much, and her decision to be nice started fraying at the edges. Why was Stefan suddenly the one who mattered?

"Yes, you can take it off," said Stefan.

Judy took a deep breath and tried again.

"It really is kind of you, Stefan, but it is so much work. Why don't you just put it back together again now? I mean, we've already been here a long time, putting Farmor to all that trouble…"

Stefan sighed.

"If I put it together now it is not finished."

"But it will go, won't it?"

"Yes, it will go."

"So why not put it back together?"

"Because every time I look at it I will not see a camper van. I will see a rusty brake cylinder behind the rear left wheel, or a cracked bushing sleeve, or a worn fuel lead, or something. If I know it is there I will see it in here." He pointed at his head. "I do not want these things in here."

"But you won't have to look at the van. We'll be gone."

Stefan turned away and pulled his mask down.

"Don't look at the flame, please." and said gruffly. "Mask, William."

He picked up the welding torch, adjusted the mixture, reached into his pocket for the lighter, and went back to work.

Judy stood there for a moment. Well, what was that all about? Why was he suddenly playing taciturn Swedish peasant? She stomped back to the house, and went back to her reading.

The truth of the matter was that Stefan was easily put out by this girl who had shown up in the middle of the night in the weirdest of circumstances and now sat reading Farmor's books or skiing around the countryside. She was not like anyone he had met before. She made him uncertain, and he wasn't used to being uncertain.

He and Farmor knew most of the story now. Even if Judy had wanted to keep it a secret, there was William – who could no more keep a secret than he could stand on a pair of skis, and he definitely couldn't do that. So Stefan knew about Judy's father, and that they had sort of escaped from England so that Judy wouldn't end up being taken away. It wasn't very odd, then, that she had a lot to think about and was sometimes a bit prickly. No, the thing that made Stefan unsure of himself was that she was so different from the people he knew. She not only looked different, but was different. He had lots of friends and knew everybody – really *everybody* – who lived in the area, and she wasn't like any of them. He knew most of the time what people were thinking; what they said didn't surprise him much. But he never knew what Judy was going to say – whether she was going to laugh at something, or make those eyebrows of hers into a v-shape and say something sharp. And he had to admit to himself that he looked forward to the evening meal a lot. William and Judy had all sorts of weird conversations, and Stefan needed a lot of help from Farmor to keep up with them, but he really liked listening to them. And something had happened to Farmor, too. She talked a lot more. She said her English was coming back, but it wasn't just that. She was chatty and lively – she even made silly jokes sometimes, and then looked a bit embarrassed; and funnily enough, she even seemed younger. Anyway, when Judy reminded him that they would be gone soon, and the sooner the better as far as she was concerned, Stefan remembered that he would get back to his ordinary life: the quiet evening meals when nothing much was said, the work of the farm, school. He found that he wasn't especially pleased about that.

At suppertime the following evening, there was some strange news. Farmor had got a phone call to say that Mr Balderson had disappeared. Apparently he had opened his eye, sat up in his hospital bed, removed a lot of apparatus from his arms and his nose and just walked out into the night. They were worried about him, of course, but Judy wasn't.

"I expect he'll show up sooner or later," she said.

"He's probably immortal."

"I think I must stay and work on the van tomorrow," said Stefan. "Because then you can leave soon, if your friend comes."

He looked at Judy and she looked back at him but said nothing.

Farmor said something, though. It was in Swedish, and there was quite a lot of it. Whatever it was, it made Stefan look down at his plate. They cleared the table and Judy tried to help with the washing-up but was shooed away by Farmor, so she went into the sitting-room and sat down on the rug in front of the tiled stove. The small brass doors were open and birch wood flamed and crackled on a bed of glowing coals, radiating heat into her face. Judy felt bad. She had made trouble between Stefan and his Farmor, because she was desperate to get away, to be doing something, anything. She hadn't understood what Farmor had said but it was plain enough. He had been going to bunk off school to get the work done as soon as possible, and Farmor wasn't having any of that. She should never have gone into the workshop and showed how impatient she was to leave. She had put her foot in it with Stefan. He couldn't do a half-decent job even if he wanted to, so now he was going to work even harder. It was all a mess, and there was no logic to any of it.

In Stefan's room William was on the floor, lying on his mattress and leafing through an old leather-bound volume that he had found in the living room, where there were ten of them in a row. It was some kind of encyclopaedia, and among the closely written texts were old, black-and-white photographs. Some were of interesting things. He had found a picture of stern-looking men with moustaches and waistcoats standing on the bank of a wide river. Several of them were holding long poles, topped by hooks exactly like the one he had found.

Stefan was sitting at his little table with a pencil in his hand and a school textbook open in front of him. William heard a sigh and a muttered Swedish word that Stefan had told him never to use in front of Farmor, although Stefan had used it at least twice in the workshop. It was a bit odd to see those wide shoulders and that broad back all hunched up. One elbow was on the table and the left hand, with its work-flattened finger-tops, grimy nails and a big scar across the base of the thumb, was pressed up to his head.

Stefan felt William's gaze on him and looked up. "Work for school."

"Homework. It's called homework. Maths."

"Yes, how do you know?"

William didn't answer that. It was so obvious. When someone who was strong and kind and could do almost everything – even rush down hills on skis – had a look on his face like that, it had to be maths.

"I'll get Judy."

William left the room, and came back a few moments later with Judy in tow. She came in and looked around. They had been there almost two weeks now, but she had never been into Stefan's room before. It wasn't the typical boy's room she had been expecting, with stuff lying about all over the place. It was neat and simple, with a chest of drawers, bed and small table, and a shelf full of books that seemed, at a quick glance, to consist entirely of manuals of various kinds. On the wall there was a small hanging cupboard. Nothing else.

Stefan looked up at her.

"William said you needed help," she sounded tired, and serious.

"No, not at all. And you cannot help. I am in final year. It is very difficult. Tomorrow is a big test."

Stefan wasn't good at being helped at the best of times. Some people are like that. He preferred to stand and fall on his own efforts. And Judy was probably at least a year younger than him, maybe even more, and she was a girl. A lot of the girls in his class sat and giggled and talked to each other in little groups and said that they didn't "get it" before the teacher had even finished explaining. And the boys weren't much better, sitting at the back and acting up, treating the girls like idiots. Most women worked much harder than most men, he knew that. And the farm would fall apart in a month if it wasn't for Farmor, no matter what Stefan did. He knew that too. But this was final year maths, and he had to get it sorted or all his plans would come to nothing. There would be no place at a decent high school, no engineering college, no helicopter pilot's license. He would be sitting in the cab of some huge harvester for the rest of his life, clear-felling the forest.

"Thank you but now I must work," he said.

Judy bit her tongue. She could see what he was thinking. He probably even had some ancient notions about girls and maths, because however kind and hospitable these people were, you couldn't exactly call them hyper-modern. It wouldn't have surprised her to hear something like "a woman's place is in the home" or "you can't expect a man to understand housework" coming out of their mouths. She thought about just leaving him to it, but to see this self-confident boy who could jump into a tractor and coax a three-ton camper out of the ditch sitting all scrunched up over some homework... It sort of got to her.

So Judy smiled, lifted her eyebrows and said in a carefully shy voice,

"Oh, is it so difficult? You must be very clever. Can I see please?" She wasn't very good at sounding cute, but she did her best, and Stefan moved his chair aside so she could see. She leant over to look at his maths book. It was algebra – mostly straightforward linear equations and simple functions.

Oh my god, thought Judy. *He's in trouble if this is too hard for him.*

How was she going to help him? How much did he understand? She knew he wasn't stupid; he must have just had rotten teachers.

"Can you show me how you do these? Please? Even if I don't understand everything."

William wandered off into the kitchen were Farmor was sitting comfortably at the table with a knitted jersey laid out in front of her.

"William, there you are," she said when she saw him. "Could you go in to the other room and see that the fire is out? Remember to poke it properly. No glowing coals. Then you can shut the doors and close the damper."

William did as he was told. An hour passed. From Stefan's room came a murmur of voices, and then a burst of laughter. Farmor frowned and stood up. Stefan was obviously not working. She was pleased that Stefan had someone to talk to, and could practise his English, but Judy mustn't disturb his work. If he was laughing, then he could not possibly be doing his homework, not Stefan.

She peeked round the door to see two heads, one dark, one light, bent over the maths book.

"It's only an identity sign; a symbol of exact balance," Judy was saying. "You can add, multiply, subtract, whatever, but if you don't do the same thing on both sides, it all goes pear-shaped."

"Pear-shaped? Not an apple or a banana? Like a pear?"

"Um, yes a pear, definitely a pear," said Judy, trying unsuccessfully to suppress a giggle.

"Now you are laughing at me. But I can speak more Swedish than you can."

"Very true, Stefan, very true. But look, all I mean is, what happens if you put more weight on one side of a flywheel than the other?"

Now it was Stefan's turn to laugh.

"I don't want to think about that. It's not very nice to think about. Pieces everywhere. Very dangerous. It happened to me once; I had to dig a bit out of the wall of the workshop. Could have chopped my head off."

"Well, there you are then. That's pear-shaped for you. Don't let it happen. Ever."

"I promise."

Farmor backed out of the room with a small smile on her face.

13

A few days later Farmor and William were at the kitchen window, looking out at the fading afternoon light. They were watching Stefan coming up the track from the road where the school bus had left him. Farmor narrowed her eyes.

"It went well, I think. But if you could go and let Silla out we will soon be sure."

William went out into the hall and opened the door for the elkhound Silla, who had been curled up asleep on the doormat. She shot off like a rocket down the track, barking.

Back in the kitchen, they watched her skid to a halt in front of Stefan.

"Now," said Farmor, "let's see."

Silla sank to a low crouch in front of Stefan, with her belly almost on the snow and her tail waving. Stefan crouched down and said something. With a yelp the dog threw herself at him and he rolled on to his back, with the dog on top of him. A wrestling match had started.

Farmor turned from the window. "Oh yes," she said. "It went well."

When Stefan came in, he was red-faced from his fight with Silla, but trying to look serious. It didn't work. He couldn't control the wide smile that lit up his face.

"Hello. I'm back."

Judy was sitting by the stove, with a Swedish grammar book open on her knee; she had decided to pass the time usefully and was learning the language, with Farmor's help. She looked up coolly, giving a very good impression of not being particularly interested.

"Hi, Stefan."

Stefan walked over to her.

"Ask me, please. Ask me how the test went."

"Oh yes, the test. You were getting the results today, weren't you? Was it OK?"

"It went well. It went very well. I did not go pear-shaped."

"Good. No mistakes then? You got all of them right?"

"All? All? Are you a mad person? Nobody gets them all right."

Judy couldn't help herself. "I do."

Stefan gave Judy what was meant to be a playful slap on the shoulder, but it caught her off balance and almost knocked her off her chair.

"Stefan!" said Farmor sharply, and started telling him off properly. She was pretty hard on him, Judy's few words of Swedish picked up that much, including "idiot", which is almost the same in Swedish as in English, and finally "woodshed". But Farmor's hard words had no effect at all on Stefan. In fact he gave her a big hug before disappearing into the hall humming to himself.

"He must go to the woodshed and use up some energy," said Farmor. And soon after that the muffled *thunk* of the axe on the block told them that he was doing just that.

Judy went to the sitting-room to be around the

books. For once she was not thinking about her father, but about William. It didn't seem to bother him much, but they would have to get some sort of message to his mother so she knew he was all right. She didn't seem to be a very motherly type, admittedly, leaving him on his own at Christmas and all that, but surely she'd be more than worried by now? Farmor could write a letter and say that he was staying with her, that was the best way. They didn't have to bring up Mr Balderson and the camper. Judy sighed. Poor William. What on earth was going to happen to him? He was hopelessly dependent on the people around him, and yet so completely himself. He would never just put on a personality to suit other people – he couldn't even if he wanted to. It was everybody else who did. That was how you survived, how you fitted in. The biggest part of everybody was hidden inside them. The bit you saw was the bit they thought you would like, or the bit they dared to show you, or maybe even a completely made-up bit that had nothing to do with them at all. But William, well, "what you see is what you get" fitted him perfectly.

He reminded her of the stories her father loved to tell about Mullah Nasruddin – the *idiot savant* he called him, the clown of God.

Stefan put his head round the door, came over to the sofa. He took a deep breath, and came straight to the point, looking at a spot just above her head.

"Hello, Judy. I am sorry that I hit you."

Judy looked up at him.

"You mean Farmor is sorry that you hit me."

Stefan grinned.

"Yes, mostly. I did not hit you very much. But I am a little bit sorry if I made you sad."

"You didn't."

"Good. Then I'm not much sorry at all."

Judy laughed.

"Right, I'm glad that's sorted out."

Stefan had something in his hand. Now he opened his palm and held it out to her.

It was a small, beautifully painted fish, an exact replica of something – a little trout, perhaps, judging by the delicate spots and the roseate colour along its sides. At first Judy thought it was an ornament, or a pendant or earring of some sort. Then she saw the barbed hooks dangling from its tail and under its belly.

"It is a wobbler," said Stefan. "A floater. Of course you cannot use it now. Not for ice-fishing. But in the spring. For you."

"For me?"

"Hold it carefully. If you get a hook in you it is hard to get out. You must cut yourself open with a knife."

Judy had never been fishing in her life, but she knew a real present when she saw it – something that has real value both for the giver and the receiver.

She looked at it closely.

"It's beautiful. But… You've said sorry. And it was no big deal, you really don't have to…."

Stefan smiled.

"But it is not for the hit. For the maths."

"Oh…" said Judy. "Then, thank you, Stefan."

"It is good, yes? Better than in a shop."

"You *made* it?"

"Yes, of course I made it," said Stefan.

Judy looked at the perfectly shaped little fish, the delicately painted eyes, fins and tail, the little scooped piece of copper fastened under the head so that it would move through the water like a living thing. How could those hands have done this?

"I can't take this from you. It's too good for me. I mean … it needs to be used, not just looked at."

"Do not worry, we have lots of rods; in the spring…"

He stopped abruptly. Spring was months away.

"I think in England there are fish," he finished lamely.

14

Stefan had announced the previous evening that he would have to go into the village to look for a piece for the camper at the scrapyard. Over breakfast the following morning he tried to explain what it was, and why it was past repair on the camper and had to be replaced. He talked at length about gussets, side rails and tower braces. He had looked up the words in one of his manuals the night before, but it didn't help. Neither William nor Judy understood a word of it.

"But I am talking English!" he exclaimed.

"It's not English to me, Stefan, sorry," said Judy.

"There is room for someone of you to come with me. Help me to look."

Judy waited for him to tell William to go and get ready.

"Please come, Judy. It might be a bit boring for you though."

The idea that anything that got her out for a bit could be boring was so ridiculous that Judy laughed.

"I think I can take it. I can always bring a book."

Stefan looked doubtful.

"If you would like to stay here and read…"

"No, no, for heaven's sake, I was just—"

"Making a joke?"

"Yes."

Stefan frowned. He was trying to understand the English way of making little jokes all the time, but he still got tripped up. He had learnt something though; understanding a language was not the same thing as understanding the people who spoke it. He needed Judy to come because she was so unbelievably quick at working stuff out, and if he could only explain exactly what he was looking for, dimensions, curvature, she would see straight away if it would do the job. And he wanted to show off his car. It was a Volvo PV 544 that he had spent many long hours converting into an A-tractor registered farm truck, and it was the envy of the village. Theoretically it had a maximum speed of thirty kilometres an hour, but just like every other converted car in the Swedish countryside, that was theory. And he wasn't actually old enough to drive it off the property, not quite. But this was the only thing that Farmor turned a blind eye to. She pretended not to know about the licensing age for farm vehicles, and he had never made a point of informing her.

So that morning when Judy stepped outside she was confronted by the sight of a gleaming red vehicle, glinting in the morning sun. It had obviously once been an ordinary old-fashioned car. But it had been transformed. The back half had been shortened and replaced by a small flatbed; there were only two front seats for passengers. Everything that was not shining red was gleaming chrome. The tires were whitewalls, the rear suspension was raised, and the front almost stroked the ground. Judy was reminded of pictures of drag racers.

Stefan stood beside it, trying to look nonchalant.

Judy knew what was expected of her instantly, and this time there would be no mistakes.

"Stefan, what an incredible car. You cannot possibly have bought this in a shop. Where did you get it?"

"I got it from an old farmer; it was behind his barn in the nettles. Very rusty, very bad."

"You mean you did all this yourself? It's unbeliev-able. It's beautiful." She was flattering him, but she meant every word of it, and Stefan could see that.

"But I must have better exhaust pipes. It is too quiet."

"Too quiet?"

"Yes, it must make a noise and make people angry. My friend's is noisier. Now get in please."

Judy climbed into the front seat and Stefan got behind the wheel. When he started the engine, it emitted a growling roar that would have done justice to a heavy goods vehicle on a steep uphill gradient. And then they were off.

It was a clear day. The village lay about twelve kilometres from Stefan's home, along the same winding, tree-lined road that they had driven up in the freezing dark the night of their crash. Now, with the sun shining through the breaks in the trees, and birch saplings and scrubby alder bowed down almost to the ground under their great hoods of snow, it was beautiful. As the sun rose, the light became stronger and the snow was almost too bright to look at. Stefan showed off a bit, accelerating to almost fifty kilometres an hour, and going into a deliberate skid in the corners. Judy grabbed hold of the seat, but she didn't say anything. If he thought he could make her start screeching then he had another think coming. They rounded the last bend and the forest fell away to reveal open meadows sloping down to the river, dotted with the occasional red-painted timber barn, and a few farmsteads. Further away, Judy could see the onion dome of the church bell tower, standing separately from the church building itself. They drove down the main street of the village, and Stefan lifted his hand in greeting to almost everybody he saw, or so it seemed to Judy. There was a general store, a petrol station and a café in the village, and that was about it. Stefan drove them over a bridge then swung off the road and up a rough track where they arrived at a pair of wire-mesh gates. Stefan stopped the car and got out, so Judy followed him, and they walked through the gates and into the scrapyard. She looked around her. Stefan was already wandering about, brushing snow off wrecked cars, bits of farm machinery and scrap iron. The place was filled with old boilers, tin roofing, a whole mountain of wheels and hubcaps, pipes, radiators... There was no end to it.

The weather wasn't too bad – it probably wasn't much below minus ten – but there is nothing colder than scrap iron. The cold that seemed to hang around the abandoned metal objects of the scrapyard soon chilled Judy to the bone. She rounded an ancient decaying combine harvester, almost completely invisible under its icy coat, and saw Stefan deep in conversation with a stooped figure dressed in a filthy overall and a greasy peaked cap. Apparently immune to the cold, he wasn't wearing a coat. The sight made Judy shiver. They were studying a twisted piece of steel girder that lay on the ground between them. Stefan saw Judy and called her over.

"I think this is good. It is three-millimetre steel."
She came over and looked down at it. Stefan had given her a piece of paper in the car with the measurements and the rough curvature he was looking for.

"Yes, it will hold. But you'll have to reshape one end for a good fit."

"No I won't."

"How much do you bet?"

"I don't want to take money from you."

"You don't want to lose it, you mean."

"Ha! Five crowns, then."

"You're on. Let's go, Stefan, I'm freezing to death."

They loaded their find on to the back of the car, and drove back towards the village, but Stefan stopped the car just before the bridge.

"Now we have a piece of cake and a cup of coffee at the café," he said.

"Are we going to walk from here?"

"Yes. When we drove in I saw Sven in the café. He is the policeman."

Judy waited, her eyebrows making a question.

"If he doesn't see me drive, it is all right. And he

has not seen me. But if I park outside the café, he must do something, and he doesn't want to make Farmor unhappy. It is not good for him."

"Why not?"

"His wife is Farmor's best friend."

So they walked.

The café was warm, with a few small tables and a glass-fronted counter with cinnamon buns, cream cakes, and a lot more besides. Judy had already discovered that Stefan had a sweet tooth, when she had seen him wolf down eight or nine of Farmor's cinnamon buns in one sitting, and now she saw him choose a slab of marzipan-coated cream cake. She contented herself with a bun, and practised her Swedish on the lady behind the counter, managing "Hello" and "One of those please" and getting a reply that she didn't really understand. At a table by the window a grey-haired man in uniform was drinking coffee and idly leafing through the newspaper. He greeted Stefan and asked him a question. Stefan replied with the odd upward jerk of the head and indrawn breath, between pursed lips, that passes for "yes" in the North. There were other people at the tables and most of them said something to Stefan. Nobody met Judy's eye, but she could feel eyes on her back as they sat drinking their coffee.

"I don't think they like strangers," said Judy as they were walking back over the bridge.

"They don't know you, that's all."

They crossed the bridge and got back to the car. Judy was already in the passenger seat, and Stefan was opening the door on his side when they heard someone shout Stefan's name. Three people were on the bridge walking towards them. One of them waved a hand. Stefan lifted a hand in reply, then walked back on to the bridge to meet them. Judy stayed in the car and watched, sinking down a bit in her seat. She might be a thousand miles from home, but her visit to the café had reminded her that she was basically on the run. If people noticed her too much, why shouldn't they start asking questions, and making phone calls? There were two girls and a boy as far as she could make out, though their down parkas and boots made it hard to tell. About Stefan's age, school friends probably. The four of them stood for a while talking. Then the boy laughed and pointed at the truck. Stefan said something, and quite suddenly the atmosphere changed. The boy moved up very close to Stefan. Stefan took a step back, shrugged his shoulders and turned to go. But Judy knew it was too late for that. She could read the signs. The boy grabbed Stefan's arm, swung him round, and took a wild swing at him with his other arm. Stefan half-ducked, avoiding the worst of the blow. He pushed his open hand into the boy's face, punched him in the neck, and then moved round quickly to get an arm round his throat and a knee in his back. They were fairly evenly matched. Stefan's opponent was shorter than him, but broad and long in the arm.

The fight seemed to have blown up out of nowhere. Judy really did not want to get involved, it wasn't her business; and if you want to avoid drawing attention to yourself then you can't just turn up among complete strangers and get straight into a punch-up. Anyway, Stefan seemed to be doing all right; he was no William. In fact at this moment his opponent was on his back on the gritted icy surface of the bridge with Stefan sitting on top of him holding his arms down. The two girls had been standing to one side, not egging the fighters on exactly, but not trying to stop them either. But now one of them yelled, picked up a lump of frozen snow from the side of the road and advanced towards Stefan. She lifted it high, but before she could bring it down on Stefan's head both her feet were swept from under her and she landed with an audible *thump* on her bottom. She squirmed round to find a black-haired, flashing-eyed figure standing quite still, balancing on her toes, knees slightly bent, staring down at her.

"Sorry," said Judy, trying to sound nice. "But that isn't fair, we should stay out of it. Let me help you up." And she stretched out a hand. This didn't seem to satisfy the girl. She screamed something at Judy, scrambled up and launched a kick at her with her booted foot. But her foot, somehow, got itself stuck under Judy's arm. And now, as Judy moved forward, she had to hop backwards, arms flailing in order to avoid landing on her bottom again. The bridge had a low metal rail, half-hidden under a hard ridge of old ploughed snow. The girl was pushed back towards it, bouncing idiotically on one leg. Her attacker gave a final heave, jerked the captured boot upwards, and with a high-pitched howl the girl flipped backwards and disappeared. Her companion let out a yell and rushed off the bridge to flounder down through the deep snow to the riverbank. This put a stop to Stefan's fight. He climbed off the boy he was sitting on, who stood up and brushed grit and snow off himself. They saw Judy, with one knee on the rail, peering over the edge, and went to join her. All three of them looked down. The river had been frozen over since before Christmas, and deep untouched drifts of snow lay on the ice. The girl whom Judy had unceremoniously dumped was half-crawling, half-wading through the drifts towards the bank, looking like an animated snowman and trying to wipe snow out of her face. On the bank stood her friend, still producing an unbroken flood of hysterical Swedish, until the boy on the bridge shouted something at her. She glared up at him, but shut her mouth.

"Now we go," said Stefan.

*

On the way back Stefan said nothing for a long time. Judy sat and stared out of the window as the pine-trunks slid past, an unbroken phalanx like soldiers on parade. She was annoyed with herself. The sitting-it-out bit hadn't gone very well. She really had to stop chucking people into canals and rivers. She wondered what Stefan would think of her – probably not a lot, just when things had started to be easier between them; almost as though she had a friend. And now this. Beating up his schoolmates wasn't going to go down well. Stefan spoke at last,

"You are a pretty strong person."

"No I'm not; you don't have to be strong, it's not about muscles."

"I know that. I mean strong in the soul."

Judy had got used to Stefan and Farmor talking about soul – apparently all Swedes did. They didn't mean anything to do with angels and heaven, or life after death. The "soul" was everything inside you that wasn't just your brain – all the stuff that made you a person and not a computer, all the stuff that messed you up.

"I don't know about that. But I know I lose my temper sometimes."

"Anna was lucky."

"Lucky?"

"Yes, going off the bridge is not good."

"But it was like landing on a feather bed."

"The water moves very fast under the bridge. Sometimes it hardly freezes at all. Or melts under, with the snow on top so you can't see it. If it was a bit later, a few weeks maybe with some good weather, Anna would be dead. Pulled under the ice by fast water. It has happened before."

"Oh."

"You didn't know that?"

"No, how could I?"

"I thought because you are so clever, perhaps you could think it."

"No."

"But if you had thought it … that it might be very bad for her … would you…?"

"No, of course not… I mean, I don't think so. I hope not."

"Is that what it is like when you lose your temper?"

Judy turned her head and looked at him – his brow wrinkled, blue eyes on the road ahead, jaw pushed forward making lines at the side of his mouth. Was it possible that she was sitting beside someone who had never lost his temper? Then Stefan's brow cleared, and he laughed out loud.

"Anna called you a mad witch. Ha ha. Very scared. She never met some girl like you. Ha ha."

"What was it all about, anyway?"

"Just stupid stuff. Look, big tracks. Some elk crossed the road here."

Talk about changing the subject, thought Judy. Not very subtle. She remembered the boy laughing and pointing towards the truck.

"It was about me, wasn't it?"

"Just stupid stuff. My friend Karl is quite stupid. His grandfather is not so nice. Karl just talks after him, like a…" Stefan's English collapsed. "A bird that talks."

"A parrot."

"Yes, a parrot."

"So, what were they saying? How did they even know I'm here?"

221

"Here everybody knows everything. Don't worry."

Judy got annoyed.

"Stop trying to look after me. I can look after myself. What is the matter with you? You get me into a fight and then you won't even tell me what it was about. "

"I did not get you into a fight."

"Yes you did."

"You were in the truck. I never tell you to come out."

"Is that what you would have done, just sat and watched?"

"No, but you're a…"

"Don't say it or I really will lose my temper. That stuff on the bridge will seem like a vicar's tea party."

"A what, please? I don't understand vicars."

Judy laughed.

"Who does?"

They drove on in silence. Already the light was going; the shadows of the trees reached right across the road and far into the forest on the other side. Stefan took a deep breath.

"Here in Sweden now lots of people come from wars and bad things. Some people say it is too many. They use rude words. The government sends many of them up here. People here are good people, but they are not used to it, and some have bad ideas from long ago. Karl's grandfather in the War… Farmor will not tell me, but she doesn't like him very much…" Stefan's voice trailed away. "Karl said something stupid. He often does. Then I said something back."

Judy stared out of the window. Why should it be different here? William's Jerry was everywhere. Just another name and another country.

"And you, what do you think?"

"My Farmor came from Finland in a row-boat, six year old. Her grandfather the Russians took away. Her father died in the war. Her uncle died in the boat."

"So why would you call a person like Karl your friend? He tried to beat you up."

"You don't understand. We go fishing. I fix engines with him. We play hockey and sit in the sauna after. But sometimes friends fight. This is where we live."

Judy sort of understood. It wasn't like living in a big city. It was hard to imagine walking down the street and knowing every face, and being known, but she guessed it wasn't all bad. It had probably saved them from dying in that frozen ditch.

Stefan went on: "There is a place for them, for the new people, not far from here, where they stay. The government puts them there; Karl said…"

Judy gasped and stared at Stefan. "An asylum centre! Stefan, the letter must have come from there, it must have! Rashid was there, it's obvious. He might still be there."

"It is possible. When a person is in there it is not so easy for them to get back out again. Sometimes a year, sometimes even two, waiting to hear if they will stay, or be sent back. But your father… I don't understand."

"Nor do I. But I bet he went there. And even if he got Rashid out and went off somewhere, somebody will know something. We must go there."

"Yes, we will go there."

"Can't we go now?"

"No, I am sorry."

"But you said it wasn't far from here."

"Yes, not far. About a hundred kilometres."

Judy sighed. "Not far" meant something very different in Scandinavia.

15

Now that Judy had something to hope for, something that might really lead somewhere, it was even harder just waiting around – waiting for the camper to be fixed, waiting to see if Mr Balderson would show up, if he ever did. And with Mr Balderson out of action, who would drive her to the asylum centre even when Stefan *did* finish working on the van?

"I cannot drive you there in the truck," Stefan had said. "There is another policeman who is not Sven. Farmor does not sew clothes with the wife of the policeman who is there."

Judy knew she didn't want to get Stefan into trouble, so she started planning how to get to the asylum centre on her own. There must be a bus from the village. Or maybe she could just get a lift. The evening after their return from the village, she pulled on a jacket and stuffed her feet into a pair of clogs – there were always some in the hallway – and went over to the workshop to ask Stefan about it. There he was, with William at his side as usual. This time they didn't look like aliens, more like figures from an old war film in gasmasks and boiler suits. A compressor was hammering away, and Stefan was busy spraying an undercoat on one of the side panels of the camper. He caught sight of her, turned the compressor off, and took off his mask.

"You should not—"

"I know, I know, if I don't go blind I will be poisoned and get fumes in the head."

"Yes, not good for someone who has a big head like yours."

Judy picked up a work glove that was lying on the bench and threw it at him. He ducked.

"And has a temper also."

Now William piped up from under his mask.

"It's not nice to call Judy a big-head."

"Why is it not nice?" wondered Stefan. "She has a big head full of brains."

"In English it means stuck up," said Judy helpfully. "You know, too proud."

"Oh. No, Judy, you are not stuck. But perhaps you have a swollen brain. It might burst out."

Stefan reached into the pocket of his overall, and slapped five Swedish crowns on to the workbench.

"You were right. I had to reshape the side-rail. Why are you always right? Not just sometimes, but always. It is not good for you."

Judy took a deep breath and looked Stefan in the eye.

"Look, Stefan, I really need to get to that asylum centre and ask around. I just have to. I thought maybe a bus or something—"

Stefan interrupted her.

"—William, could you please go and fill the wood box for Farmor? It was almost empty." Happily William did as he was told. When they were alone, Stefan walked over to the stove and poked wood into it. Judy waited. He had something on his mind, that was clear enough.

"What's up, Stefan?"

"I want to say something to you." He fanned out a set of feeler gauges and started carefully wiping them off one by one.

"Well, say it then."

Once Stefan had started it all came out in a rush.

"I will drive you to the asylum centre tomorrow but you must please not tell Farmor because she will be unhappy and if they stop me and she does not know anything about it, and Sven will not say to Margareta that Farmor let me go there but it was only me being bad and Sven will be angry with me because he knows that I drive in the village and does not stop me and I will have broken his … his … trust but he won't be angry with Farmor."

Judy knew Stefan a lot better now than she had a few weeks ago. So she knew that this thing he was offering her meant more than even the fishing tackle. She desperately wanted to get to the asylum centre, and if anyone else had made the offer then she would have jumped at it. But she couldn't do that to Stefan.

"Stefan, have you ever lied to Farmor before?" she asked him

Stefan looked up at last. "Of course."

"When?"

He frowned, then his brow cleared and he said proudly,

"There is a place on the river where the water is very fast. I was not allowed to fish there, but I did, and I almost fell in, but I didn't tell her."

"How old were you, Stefan?"

"Six."

"Sorry, that doesn't count. Thanks a lot, Stefan, really, thanks. But not everybody's cut out for serious lying; some are, some aren't. You aren't."

"But you could help me, you have…"

"Had a lot of practice? I wish you hadn't said that, but it is true. Anyway, I'm not going to give you lessons, so forget it."

Stefan grinned.

"But you taught me maths. You are a good teacher, I won't go pear-shaped."

"Pack it in, Stefan."

"Pack it? Pack what? Pack what into what, please?"

Judy was beginning to suspect that his English wasn't as bad as he liked to pretend.

The smile left Stefan's face and he gestured towards the camper.

"Not so long now. You see we are painting. But the clutch is not quite good. The discs…"

"But, Stefan, you had the clutch out days ago, I know you did."

"Yes, but the alignment, sometimes you must do things again. You will not go alone on a bus. Mr Balderson will come back, I will finish the work, you will go and look for your father." Stefan put his mask back on and turned on the compressor; its stuttering rattle made all further conversation impossible.

Judy trudged back to the house. Hurrying was something that Stefan just didn't do, and she would only make him unhappy if she went on at him. She decided to ask Farmor for help.

Farmor happily turned her attention to Judy's problem. She could see that the girl was going mad with impatience, and she knew perfectly well that Stefan was fully capable of doing something stupid to help her. She let him drive around locally in his various vehicles, and Sven kept an eye on him, but she couldn't have him haring off a hundred kilometres. So she made a call to Stefan's uncle Jonas. When she spoke to him he said that he would be going to pick up some feed for his livestock later that week, and would pass by the asylum centre. But he could just as well go tomorrow, and anyway he needed to chat with Stefan. So the next morning a beaten-up pickup drove up to the house, and Farmor called Judy out of her room. A bandy-legged man in overalls, with a baseball cap on his head and cheerful blue eyes, stood talking to Stefan in the yard. He nodded at Judy, and gestured to the truck. Judy got in, and then to her surprise Stefan jumped in beside her.

"Are you coming too?"

"Yes I am. You do not know people or talk good Swedish and Jonas needs to speak with me for a dance in the village."

"Are you going dancing with your uncle?"

"No." Judy waited but apparently Stefan was finished.

The drive was a long one, and the truck an old one, with lots of noises from the engine and other bits, and Stefan and his uncle talked fast in the thick dialect of the area that even Swedes from the south had difficulty understanding. Judy watched the forest slide past, absorbed in all the questions that might – just might – soon be answered.

At last the road led along the bank of a wide frozen river, and Jonas turned off between two ancient knotted pines up what must once have been a fairly stately driveway. The building they came to was stone-built, stuccoed and imposing. It had been the main offices of a water-powered sawmill built at the turn of the previous century. It stood on the bank of the river, and in years gone by the timber had been floated down from many miles inland, gathered behind the booms that stretched from bank to bank, and channelled into the mill itself, where the great frame saws were waiting to deal with it. It had been in use until only a few decades before. Since then the big house had been a hotel, then divided into flats before finally being boarded up. No business could resist the pull of the big cities, so slowly but surely every one had left this quiet place and now there was little work to be had.

But now, it seemed, people were returning. From the terrorized and war-torn corners of the world, they washed up here, like flotsam after a storm, shivering in the unaccustomed cold and wondering how to make a new life, receiving whatever charity the government was prepared to give them. The old works office had been rented by the local council to make a holding centre, a place where refugees could be kept during the long process of deciding whether their lives had been awful enough for them to be allowed to stay.

The pickup came to a halt in front of the main door. The original owner of the mill, one of the rich timber barons of the nineteenth century, had wanted to make an impression. There was a pillared portico, with a flight of stone steps leading up to it. But the paint on the tall double doors was peeling, and what had once been a moulded doorframe had been roughly repaired with cement. Judy looked at the doors with a knot in her stomach. If Rashid was here then she might, in a few minutes, know where her father was, what had happened to him. In five minutes – after months of ignorance and uncertainty.

She opened the cab door and climbed down. Stefan made to follow her.

"You can stay here; you don't have to come."

"But I am coming." And Judy realized that she would be glad of some company.

They walked up the steps. There was no bell but the door was ajar, so they pushed it open and walked into a long entrance hall with a linoleum floor. At the end they could see a stairwell with doors leading off on both sides. They heard a murmur of voices from behind the door on the right, so Judy opened it.

She entered what had once been a spacious reception room, with tall windows looking out over gardens and the river, and a high ceiling. It was easy to imagine a big mahogany desk, some comfortable leather armchairs, and a cabinet of books. Now the furniture consisted of a few tables and chairs that had probably been thrown out after some office or school renovation, and an old stained sofa against one wall. On the sofa sat a woman in a hijab with two children, one no more than a baby. By the windows a group of young black men stood chatting. At one of the tables, two older men sat opposite each other in quiet conversation.

Judy stepped in. Faces turned to her, questions were asked in a variety of languages, none of which she understood. One of the men at the table pushed his chair back and came towards her, smiling. Then suddenly all voices were stilled. There was silence. The man who was approaching her with outstretched hand returned to his table, the young men turned to look out of the window, the woman on the sofa bent her head over her youngest child.

Stefan had come in.

He smiled, said hello in rather a loud voice, but there was no response. He said,

"We are looking for a person…"

The silence was complete. All faces were closed.

"Stefan, go back outside."

"But I am with you."

"Please."

Stefan stood stubbornly in the doorway for a moment. Then he went. Judy knew that he was upset, but she thought, "Well, now you know what it is like; walking into a room full of people who don't see you, who don't know that you punched your best friend for my sake, who see only the colour of your eyes, your hair, the clothes you wear, the language you speak."

The atmosphere relaxed. Judy said,

"Does anybody here speak English?"

The other man at the table stood up. Greying hair, droopy moustache, a lot of wrinkles on his forehead. He came forward.

"I do. Do you need help, have you just arrived? Where are you from?"

"No, I don't need help, thank you. I am a British citizen."

He looked at her, said something over his shoulder. A murmur went round the room, and all faces turned towards her. Judy, the lucky one, the possessor of pure gold – a European passport.

"Congratulations. But why are you here?"

"I am looking for someone."

A babble of voices as the information was translated and passed round. Everyone wanted to help. They knew what it was like. These days, it seemed, everybody was looking for someone – an uncle, a husband, a mother, a child.

"His name is Rashid."

Rashid! They are delighted – Rashid is here! In this very place! Judy's heart skipped a beat, and then started thumping so hard that she was sure they must hear it. A young man from the group at the window was despatched immediately. He left the room at a run crying, "Rashid! Rashid!" and Judy heard him leaping up the stairs, still calling.

Less than a minute passed, though to Judy it felt much longer. She was surrounded by expectant, happy smiles. Their joy was all for her, and Rashid.

The youth returned. Holding his hand was a young boy, hardly more than ten years old, with short-cropped dark hair. He was wearing a tracksuit that was too big for him, and dirty trainers. His huge eyes gazed at Judy.

Judy stared at him as her hopes crumbled. She shook her head.

"I'm sorry, I should have said. I'm looking for a grown man."

The boy Rashid still had not taken his eyes off her. He said in Farsi,

"Who are you? You are not my sister."

Judy replied in the same language.

"No, I'm not. I'm so sorry."

The boy didn't cry. He didn't seem to react at all. Perhaps in his eyes a little flame flickered and died, but that might just have been a trick of the light. He took his hand from the older boy's, turned round and walked out.

There was nothing to be said. They had all seen hopes raised and dashed, many times.

"I... Good luck. Thank you," was all Judy could say before she turned and fled. Stefan was standing at the bottom of the steps kicking irritably at a lump of old grey snow. He looked up when she came out. He didn't need to ask. They walked over to the camper and climbed in.

Uncle Jonas put the engine into gear and they drove away.

Nobody said anything as they drove on to the

farm where Jonas was to pick up his feed. When they arrived, Jonas jumped out and went into the farmhouse.

"Now he will drink coffee," said Stefan. "It will not be fast. We can fetch the bales."

The barn was huge, with sweet-smelling hay stacked almost to the roof. They started grappling bales towards the door of the barn. Judy had still not said a word. When Stefan said they had enough, she sat down on the nearest bale and stared at the floor.

Stefan placed himself in front of her.

"I know you are not happy now," he began.

Judy snorted, and bit her tongue, to stop herself making some snide comment. It wasn't Stefan's fault.

"Please listen to me. Your father's friend could still be in the area. Staying in town, perhaps. If he got his... If he was allowed to stay, he can find a flat, even a job maybe."

"If he got his residence permit he could be anywhere in the country, couldn't he?"

"Yes, but many stay here, if they have got to know

someone, or found a friend."

"Low probability."

"Judy, this is not maths. You make me…"

"Pissed off?" She had got used to helping him improve his English.

"No, I want to shake you, and make all the equations fall out of your ears."

"Oh."

"You have not to lose the soul of your journey. Why give up now? It is stupid. Only a brainy person like you could be so stupid. There was almost no chance of finding your father when you started, and there is still almost no chance. So what is different? The soul of the journey is the same."

Jonas appeared before Judy could reply. They loaded the bales on to the bed of the truck, and headed back.

16

Judy spent the next day, and the day after that, on skis, covering miles, moving fast over frozen lakes and slowly through thick forest, getting lost sometimes, and having to follow her own tracks back for hours to find out where she was. Stefan's words worked their way into her. By the end of the second day, she was beginning to find her way through her disappointment. The journey wasn't over; they could go on. They could ask around in town, perhaps go to the town hall or something and get some information. Even if she spent the rest of her life wandering around the world with her strange companions, there was no reason to give up on it. Anyway, what else was there to do?

Go back to England and get taken into care? She hadn't wanted that before, and she wanted it even less now. But there was no journey at the moment, that was the main problem. Both the camper and its driver were laid up; she was totally dependent on them, and being totally dependent didn't suit her one little bit.

As it turned out, the lack of a driver sorted itself out quite quickly. A couple of days later, when Judy was out on her skis again and William was busy arranging his collection in Stefan's room, there was a knock on the door. Farmor went to open it and realized at once who it was. The tall gaunt figure with a staff in his hand, the strange assortment of clothing, and the single bright eye, which fixed on her – she had heard the descriptions but Judy and William had not prepared her for the full effect of meeting the man in person.

"Good morning, ma'am," he said. "My name is Andrew Balderson. I was informed in the village that you are harbouring two friends of mine." He swept the red bobble hat from his bald head, and made a small bow.

"Yes, yes, please come in," said Farmor, as she composed herself.

Mr Balderson settled on a chair in the kitchen while Farmor bustled about nervously making fresh coffee and arranging cinnamon buns on a plate. In the silence, Mr Balderson talked of the beauties of the winter landscape, and the warmth and friendliness of her kitchen, and asked after the young people.

"They are very good people. And for my grandson, a blessing, I think," said Farmor.

As she poured out the coffee, she saw that two fingers were missing from his left hand and noticed the fresh scar. He saw her glancing at it and said,

"Ah yes, they couldn't keep them, nor a toe or two. But it was a small price to pay. Knowledge comes at a price, as I'm sure you are aware."

"Yes, but such a night…"

"Such a night indeed. A test, a trial, but such a unique opportunity! A few fingers and toes, well, they can be spared."

There was a little log cabin that stood on its own at some distance from the other buildings. It was one of the oldest buildings on the farm and had been the smithy once, which explained why it lay to one side, for fire is fast and unstoppable if it takes hold of a wooden house whose timbers have been gently distilling their resin for two hundred years. Farmor suggested shyly that it might suit him, and took him out to see it. Inside, the hut was simplicity itself. A table of rough-hewn planks, a wooden chair, a wooden bed, and the inevitable iron stove placed on a bricked base that had once supported the smith's forge. Two small windows, and walls of unsquared logs with the flax caulking showing between them. Mr Balderson sighed with pleasure, gazed at Farmor until she got quite flustered and declared,

"*Better a house, though a hut it be,*

A man is master at home;" and then he continued,

"*Bú er betra*

þótt lítið sé

halur er heima hver"

Farmor wasn't incredibly surprised. Judy had said that Mr Balderson seemed to know most of the poetry that had ever been written, so why not the Edda? And why not in Old Icelandic?

The return of Mr Balderson solved problem number one, the driver. Problem number two was the camper, and Stefan's obsession with it. Judy was beginning to think that Stefan and William were a bit alike in many ways; maybe that was why they got on so well together. They had their interests, and they went in for them wholeheartedly, to put it mildly. Stefan was fully capable of smiling cheerfully and saying it would soon be finished and then removing some important bit and starting all over again. So when was soon? And did Stefan even know what *finished* meant?

Judy followed the narrow path that Stefan had cleared to Mr Balderson's cabin. Snow was heaped up on either side so that it was like walking in a deep ditch. Thankfully, it wasn't too cold. In fact, Judy was so used to it now that minus eight degrees felt almost balmy and Spring-like. They hadn't seen much of Mr Balderson since his return. He had eaten with them the first evening and William had been very interested in what had happened to his fingers after the doctors had cut them off; he wondered if they had been buried in a little finger grave, but Mr Balderson thought probably not. After that Mr Balderson had kept himself pretty much to himself. To Judy he seemed to have changed. He was a bit forbidding now, with his hollow cheeks and his single eye that was even more penetrating somehow. So now she knocked a bit nervously at the low wooden door and waited for a greeting before stepping in.

Mr Balderson had clearly made himself at home. He was sitting on the bed knitting – the result of a conversation with Farmor about local traditional patterns – and had got himself into the mood for his work by tying his grey hair in bunches, putting on a headscarf and borrowing a voluminous skirt that had belonged to Stefan's great-grandmother. It was made of some heavy dark woollen material and spread out on either side of him in folds. If he had shaved, then he could have been any peasant woman of the north from the last century, or maybe the one before that.

Judy sat down at the table.

"Mr Balderson…" she started.

"Anthea to you, dear, try not to disturb my state of mind," Mr Balderson interjected. "This is not easy work. This is skill of the highest order. Too loose, too tight, a single mistake, and it all must be unravelled and started again. Just imagine if life was like that."

Judy tried again.

"Farmor and Stefan are being very nice to us, but…"

"No, they are not. They are not being nice to you, or polite. They are being who they are. 'Nice' is neighbours who've lived on the same street for years and never been in each other's kitchens. 'Nice' is the shop assistant who will lose their job if they don't smile at you however tiresome you are. Our hosts are just doing what people have always done: looked out for each other. The so-called law of hospitality is a law of survival. 'Nice' is a modern invention, like nuclear fission and computers and big cities."

This was not what Judy wanted to talk about.

"Sorry. But the thing is we have to get going again. We can't stay here doing nothing. Stefan's taking for ever to get the camper fixed."

"A conscientious fellow, then."

"Conscientious? He's fanatical. I'm not saying he should be a slapdash bodger, but there are limits. Do you know what he's going to do now?"

"Well, perhaps he's being a bit extra thorough. Putting off the day when we leave."

"Why would he do that?"

Mr Balderson put his knitting aside.

"You never fail to surprise me, Judy. A head full of differential calculus and yet completely brainless." Judy decided to let that pass. "I suppose it's because of the maths. I helped him a bit, but he's all right now. It was only some basic stuff that he hadn't got straight. He quite enjoys it really."

"You think it's your mathematics he'll miss, do you?"

Judy said nothing. She didn't have time for that kind of stuff. She wanted to find out something about her father, and if it didn't happen soon she would go off her head.

"It's driving me mad, anyway. Why does he have to make everything so perfect? And Farmor's just the same. She chucked all the mats and carpets in the house out into the yard the other day, brushed them off with snow, hung them up, beat them. She was totally exhausted. They weren't even dirty. I mean, it's just so … well, fussy."

"*Fussy*? Did you say *fussy*? Wrong, Miss Azad. I must say you are not at your best. I prescribe less thinking and more seeing. Bitter experience has taught people here to take their time and get it right. Not so long ago, really, when Farmor was a child, living up here in the winter was about survival. A log cabin, a timbered farmhouse were like ships afloat on a frozen ocean: an ocean of trees. If things weren't done just right, you died. Froze to death or starved. It's still real to Farmor, the life where a bit of sloppiness can kill. A lame horse is a catastrophe. A door left open means your root store is destroyed or your calf is taken by a lynx or a wolf. Some years the crops failed – an 'unyear' they call it, did you know that? They had to grind birch-bark to make their bread. Even so, by March there were tiny coffins in the morgue at the church, waiting for the ground to thaw so that they could be buried."

Mr Balderson paused. "In my view, Judy, you

would do well to calm down a bit and recognize that you have come to a place where doing it properly still matters. And I am certainly not going to tell Stefan to get a move on."

Judy was not going to get any help here, that was clear enough. Mr Balderson's night in the snowdrift seemed to have changed him. He was fiercer. Not frightening exactly, but certainly not easy-going. He made Judy wary. She sat for a while and looked at the stove and at the neat pile of logs beside it. It was all very well for Mr Balderson, who, as far as she could tell, lived a life without ties to anything or anybody, and even for William, who lived in a world of interesting things that he had found, and didn't look ahead or back, ever. But for her it was different, wasn't it? Her life was a great big question that she had to find the answer to.

Mr Balderson had returned to his knitting, frowning and counting stitches, so Judy got up and moved towards the door.

"In the Valley of the Quest one must change one's state," said Mr Balderson as she stepped out into the snow.

As she made her way back towards the house, Judy realized that Mr Balderson was right as usual. He was really quite annoying in that way. Farmor and Stefan and William were simply not as wound up as she was, and why should they be? She couldn't make things happen any faster, and there was no point in being in a state about it. She didn't know what the valley of the quest was, but she could at least try to change her state.

Which was why some days later Judy found herself standing on a chair helping Farmor remove the curtains from the living-room windows. They needed to be washed and ironed in Farmor's opinion. They both caught sight of Mr Balderson on his way back from one of his little trips into the forest. He wore his long wide skirt, woollen cardigan and muffler, and was heading back towards his cabin with long gliding strides on a pair of ancient wooden skis that he had found in the rafters of the woodshed.

"Ah, he has returned," observed Farmor.

A raucous croaking, like a heavy smoker's throaty laugh, drew their eyes upwards. High above them a pair of ravens were at play, looping and rolling, even flipping over and flying upside down for a wingbeat or two. Then they slid down the clear air and settled on the ridge of the cabin roof, clacking their beaks, and muttering and jostling for a position close to the chimney where it was warmest. The ravens watched with beady eyes as Mr Balderson loosened his bindings, propped his skis against the cabin wall and ducked inside.

"Of course, they have come. I must tell Stefan," said Farmor. She spoke in Swedish, but Judy understood simple sentences now.

"Is he interested in birds?" asked Judy, stepping down from her stool and bundling up the last of the curtains.

"Yes. No. It is not that," said Farmor. She seemed a bit flustered. "I was talking to myself. I am alone a lot of the time, you know."

Mr Balderson joined them for supper that evening. Farmor wasn't quite at ease, jumping up from the table to fetch the salt or check the stove, but when Mr Balderson started a conversation about spinning yarn, which moved on to flax and the art of turning a plant into a tablecloth, she relaxed.

Stefan sat in silence, eating huge amounts of Farmor's famous elk rissoles. Judy started making small calculations in her head about how many calories per day he must use up in order to eat that much without getting fat. But he wasn't quite his usual self, Judy could see that. He ate at half-speed, though that was still pretty fast for a normal person, and wasn't following the conversation as he usually did, asking Farmor for translations sometimes, or adding some remark of his own.

After a while Judy said, "OK, Stefan, spit it out."

"Spit it out?" mumbled Stefan, with his mouth half-full. "No, it is very good food."

"It's what you say when … when," William began, but Judy broke in,

"He knows what it means, William, he's having us on. A bit of Swedish fun, I think."

Stefan swallowed and said to William,

"It is true, William, I was making a joke. But I will say that I think tomorrow the work will be done. That is not a joke. You can go on your journey again."

Farmor beamed with pride. Judy said how great it was and tried not show how her heart leapt at the thought of getting on the road again. William was less pleased.

"I like being here better. Can I stay?"

Farmor caught Judy's eye, and asked a silent question. Judy shook her head.

"It wouldn't work, William. We need you to come with us. You're our friend."

"I have to bring my collection."

"Of course you must," said Farmor. "I have a nice box that you can put it in."

They started preparing for departure the next morning. There was a surprising amount to do in the way of gathering their bits and pieces, and explaining to Farmor that they could only take about a quarter of the jars of jam and blackcurrant juice and pickled herring and sauerkraut and hard bread and buns that she tried to thrust on them. And there was William's collection, which had grown quite large during their stay. On a two hundred-year-old farm with outbuildings and lofts and stables, where things are very rarely thrown away, there are rich pickings for someone like William. Farmor produced a beautiful box of juniper wood with a clever sliding catch and the date 1872 carved on the lid. William was over the moon, and when Judy tried to protest that it was far too fine just to give away, Farmor only smiled and said that good craftsmanship needed to be where it was loved. And William said that Farmor was oldest and Judy probably shouldn't tell her what to do.

Stefan was in the workshop, and not even William was allowed to join him. He needed, at the end, to be alone with his work.

17

After lunch, under a blue sky with high clouds that spoke of a world at last coming back to life, Stefan drove Aristeas the camper, gleaming and even better than the day he was made, out into the yard. You could almost swear the camper was smiling, as the sun glinted on his newly chromed and polished grill, and flashed on the glass of his headlights. Stefan jumped out of the cab, and handed the keys ceremoniously to Mr Balderson, who gravely shook his hand. Judy said, "Are you sure about this Stefan? I thought the fan belt sounded a bit loose…"

Stefan bristled.

"No, it is tightened to exactly—" He stopped. "Aha! Another English joke. Perhaps the funniest joke I have ever heard. You must go on the television and be a famous joke person."

They would start early the next morning. After supper, which was a rather muted affair with nobody having much to say, Mr Balderson had disappeared to his hut, and Judy was sitting on her sofa reading when Stefan put his head round the door and announced in his most ponderous Swedish,

"Tires. You are only as safe as your tires. Tires are number one."

Judy put down her book.

"Yes, I've been thinking about that." The memory of their near-death experience on that freezing night was still all too clear. "There must be somewhere where we can get new ones fitted."

Stefan wasn't finished. He sat down on the sofa. There were apparently lots of different sorts of tires, and the choice of the right winter tires with deep treads and steel studs was not something that Stefan was prepared to leave to anyone other than himself.

"So I must come with you tomorrow, to the town. I know a place where we can get good tires."

"Oh…" Judy suddenly felt very happy about this. She turned her face away towards the window with its newly washed curtains and said the first thing that came into her head.

"Are you a birdwatcher, by the way?"

"You mean someone with…" Stefan made rings of his forefingers and thumbs and held them up to his eyes.

"Binoculars, yes."

"No."

"Then why did Farmor want to tell you about the ravens on Mr Balderson's roof?"

"I don't know." Stefan shrugged.

Stefan was so bad at lying that it was almost funny. Not as bad as William, of course, who never even tried, but pretty useless. Judy turned back to look at him.

"Yes you do."

"Yes I do, but I don't want to tell you. You might laugh at Farmor, I don't want you to laugh at Farmor."

"Stefan, I'm not… I mean, I know I make silly jokes, and I know you think that the English laugh

259

at everybody. Am I really a person who laughs at people?" Judy found that she very much wanted to know the answer. Stefan turned his head towards her and saw the question in her eyes.

"No, I was wrong to say that. I am quite a stupid person you know. You laugh at yourself and at the world but not at people.

"Farmor calls Mr Balderson the Allfather. So when the ravens came… Well, of course she said to me, *I told you so, Stefan, today Hugin and Munin came.*"

Judy looked puzzled. "I don't understand."

Now it was Stefan's turn to be puzzled.

"You know, Odin, the father of the Gods…"

Judy had heard of Odin, of course, and Valhalla, and Thor, but…

"You mean Farmor thinks…"

"I don't know what she thinks, really. But the one eye, you know. Odin only has one eye; he gave the other one to learn wisdom, the runes. And William talks about the great tree that fell, and it was an ash, and Yggdrasil, the tree of all life, is an ash tree. Odin walks the world in many disguises, he is a wanderer, like Mr Balderson, sometimes a man, sometimes a woman, and Odin knows everything: past and future, fate woven by the Norns at Mimer's well." Stefan stopped, and shrugged his shoulders again.

Judy said nothing. She certainly didn't feel like laughing. Rather it was as though the ground had just shifted a little under her feet. Stefan said,

"It is all right if I come tomorrow? The tires?"

"Yes, Stefan. It's really is very all right."

It was a beautiful day, brilliant sparkling white with the temperature creeping up towards zero, and Mr Balderson had dressed himself dramatically for the occasion. He was wearing his ankle-length greatcoat, a pair of leather boots that he had found in one of the sheds and lovingly restored with bear's grease, and his wide brimmed slouch hat, with a capercaillie feather in the hatband. His single blue eye glittered from beneath the brim. They said their goodbyes to Farmor. There were huge hugs for Judy and William; when Farmor came to Mr Balderson, though, Judy saw her drop to a little curtsey, and make an odd sign with the fingers of her left hand. Mr Balderson smiled.

"Our thanks for your kindness to the weary traveller. May you be repaid."

Then he jumped into the cab and started the engine.

"All aboard, youthful ones," he roared. "We are on the road again!"

This time it was Stefan who sat on the engine cowling between the front seats, listening carefully for telltale noises that would warn him if he had not tuned the engine to perfection. Mr Balderson drove very slowly; the road surface was as treacherous as it could be, with the thermometer hovering above freezing, so they sometimes lost their grip going uphill no matter how careful he was being. Only William was oblivious to the danger, lying on one of the couches in the living space and examining an old shoe with a birch-bark sole that he had found under a floorboard in the barn just before they left.

It wasn't a very big town. It lay on the coast of the Gulf of Bothnia, and had once been a thriving seaport, in the days when timber and tar and herring and flax had made wealthy burgers of its citizens. They drove along the harbour road, lined on the landward side with tall old wooden buildings that had once been warehouses and ships' chandlers and smokehouses, but were now mostly empty. They were well cared for, but just summer tourist attractions now, with the odd café and souvenir shop. On the seaward side the stone quay ran the full length of the road – deserted while all the yachts and launches were laid up for the winter and the occasional merchant vessel from Finland or the Baltic States couldn't get into the bay. The town wasn't nearly big enough to attract the services of the government ice-breakers that plied the waters north of the Gulf of Finland. The sea was a flat frozen plain, stretching all the way to the horizon and dotted here and there with small densely forested islands.

The road bent inland again, and they came to a collection of low metal-roofed sheds that housed a builder's yard, a wholesale agricultural supplier, a tractor repair shop and their destination, a tire service centre.

Stefan went inside, and was followed out moments

later by a young man in overalls. Together they bent down to study the camper's tires, and plenty of gruff laughter told the occupants of the cab that amusing remarks were being made about English people's cavalier attitude to driving in the snow.

Stefan opened the cab door.

"He has good tires for you, but he needs an hour or two. We can walk to a very good café with very good cakes."

So they decided that they would walk up to the council offices, to see if they could get some lead on Rashid, and then, said Stefan, there was something he wished to show them.

The visit to the council offices was a total failure. They walked into a shiny new building close to the town square and were greeted politely at the reception desk. William and Mr Balderson retired to some comfortable seats that were provided for visitors. They were both interested in the tourist brochures advertising various historical places of interest. Stefan got to work, and did a lot of talking, starting with the receptionist. In the end, by simply refusing to leave, he managed to get himself and

Judy shown into an office where a shirt-sleeved young man was sitting at a computer. But he hardly even looked up from whatever he was doing, and Stefan had to turn to Judy and say. "It is no good. They have some information here, but it is forbidden for him to say anything. He can only say when the asylum seeker has been given a…" His English failed. "A number, you know?"

"Social security number, or something like that?" said Judy

"Yes, something like that, and there is no one called Rashid…"

"Forget it, Stefan. Let's go," said Judy.

"Well, well," said Mr Balderson when they told him that they had drawn a blank, "the plot thickens." He got up from his chair. " I shall now remove myself from your company for a while. We meet at Stefan's café." He strode off.

Once outside, Judy had no desire to go anywhere in particular. There didn't seem to be any point.

Stefan turned to William.

"Now I will show you my shop. It is the best shop in this whole place."

"I didn't know you had a shop."

"Well, it isn't my shop, I just call it my shop."

"Why, if it's not your shop?"

"Because if it was my shop, that is what it would be like."

Judy was already well ahead, walking fast. Stefan caught up with her. They walked in silence for a while, then Judy spoke.

"There isn't much left to hope for now. Even if Rashid sent that letter from here, he's obviously moved on. He could be anywhere in Sweden. Anywhere on the planet, for that matter. "

Stefan said nothing. There really wasn't anything to say.

It turned out that the shop of Stefan's dreams was a sort of combined ironmonger's, tackle shop, and outdoor supplier. All the ways that anybody had ever thought of to join something to something else – nails from tiny to massive, screws, bolts, rivets, welding gear, glue for wood, glue for metal – were there to be browsed, along with all the tools that you might ever need to do it right. And of course fishing gear, including all the delicate fiddly stuff you need for tying flies; knives, axes, camping equipment, guns. To Stefan it was a treasure trove.

He stood for a moment and studied the window display – it was getting to be the time for ice-fishing, now that the snow cover was shrinking every day. He gazed longingly at a motor-driven ice bore, collapsible, relatively lightweight but with a very efficient five-inch spiral bit that would easily deal with half a metre of core ice. It was Japanese, and normally he was faithful to the quality Swedish manufacturers, but it had to be admitted that when it came to getting the balance right between weight and function, the Japanese were at the top of the heap. Judy was already inside going through a box of lures, half-price because they were out of season, and comparing them unfavourably to the one that Stefan had given her. Stefan turned to explain to William the important differences between angling under ice or on open water. But William wasn't there.

"Judy, where did William go?"

"What?" She had been miles away.

"William, did you see where he went?"

"No."

He was nowhere to be seen.

William was in the municipal museum. They had passed it on the way to Stefan's shop, and William had got distracted by it. It was housed in a noble stone-built edifice dating from the nineteenth century, and there was a poster outside showing artefacts that had been found in the local area. A burial site from the Scandinavian Iron Age had been excavated recently, and there were photographs. William stopped and studied the poster while Stefan and Judy rounded the corner and disappeared ahead of him. In no time at all he was on his way up the steps.

The first room held axe-heads and swords, and a shield-boss from the early Viking period. There was also a small model of a long-house, with the roof lifted off so that you could see the great hearth that had run almost the length of the hall, and the benches and trestle-tables where the warriors had sat draining their mead-horns and listening to the harpists sing of the deeds of their forefathers.

There were other exhibits, from the iron age or even earlier. There was one complete skeleton of an early iron-age warrior, lying as they had found him, in a reconstruction of his grave, with his sword at his side. William wandered through the rooms, totally absorbed, and was drawn to a small well-lit glass display-case. There he saw something that rooted him to the spot. On display were a silver brooch, a little pile of silver coins, a pendant of some kind that might have been a cross but wasn't quite because the arms of the cross went right across the top like a capital T. And something else. A small elongated thing, forked and bent upwards at one end, with the other end like a sort of flattened spoon.

William reached inside his shirt and drew up his find. It was bigger, and it wasn't made of silver, but it was the same shape. Not exactly the same shape, but very nearly. William peered at the neat little label that lay next to the exhibit. It was in Swedish.

He looked around. The museum was almost deserted, but he remembered seeing someone a couple of rooms back, and retraced his steps. He found a woman dressed in a housecoat and

269

headscarf pushing a cleaner's trolley laden with mops and buckets and floor-clothes and bottles of cleaning fluid in the direction of the toilets. She stopped when William came towards her. He saw that she wasn't very old – about the same age as his mother, he thought. She too had been a cleaner for a while, but she hadn't liked it very much. This lady wasn't like his mother in any other way, though. She had dark hair and eyes, more like Judy, and she looked tired.

"Can you read a label for me please?" asked William.

He wondered if she could understand him. She could.

"What label do you mean?"

"Over here." The woman followed him back to the room with the display case.

"Look," said William, holding up his find, "they're the same, and I don't know what it is, and now there's one here, though it's not *quite* the same is it?"

Now the woman smiled at him.

"Well, I can read the label for you, at least." She was quiet for a moment, mouthing the words as though the language was unfamiliar to her.

"It is a key."

"A key? But it can't be. Keys don't look like this. Have you read it right?" William was thinking of the key to the flat that he usually had round his neck at home.

"It says that the first keys looked like this. It is … let me see … about a thousand years old."

"A thousand?"

"Yes, I think so. Mediaeval, that would be about a thousand years ago."

William stared at his find, turning it over and over in his hands.

"You have made a good find, I think," the cleaning lady went on. "Did you find it here?"

"No, in England, under a big tree."

"And you have come here from England? Are you on holiday?"

"No, I came here with Judy, but it was by mistake – she's looking for someone who sent a letter, though she doesn't know much. From her father's friend, he sent it from here. But she's not really looking for him, she's looking for her father –

he went away and didn't come back. Now she's sad because Rashid wasn't at the asylum centre."

As William spoke, the woman's face had gone very still, and when he said the name Rashid, she drew a sharp breath.

"The person you came with, what is her name?"

"Judy, I told you."

"I mean her ... surname."

"Er ... Azad."

Suddenly the woman bent down and took hold of his shoulders. He didn't like it, but he didn't mind nearly as much as he used to.

"Where is she now? Please. I must talk to her."

"She's ... oh." Now William remembered that he had lost Judy and Stefan, or they had lost him.

"They were going to a shop."

Stefan and Judy retraced their steps. Somehow William had managed to disappear. Judy wasn't too worried – especially when Stefan decided that he knew where William was.

They walked back to the museum. As soon as they went in it was utterly obvious that this was where they would find William. "This is a Parkinson paradise," said Judy, gazing around at the exhibits. When they came to the third room, sure enough, there he was, apparently in conversation with the cleaning lady.

"Judy, Stefan, it's a key, I've got a key! It's a thousand years old! Look. Look in there. That one's just the same, and she says it's a key." He gestured to the woman who was standing looking at Judy as though she was afraid of her.

"Are you Judy Azad?" the lady said.

Judy sighed inwardly. Presumably William had blurted out her whole sorry tale already, to this complete stranger.

"Yes, I'm Judy."

"And you are looking for your father."

William had clearly been busy. "Yes."

"I have talked to him."

18

Judy was stunned. At last, after all this time, someone had seen her father.

"Where is he?" she blurted out. "What's happened to him?" Judy bit her tongue, trying to control her furious impatience.

"He was looking for a man called Rashid, the sender of a letter. Please come and sit down, I must explain."

They followed her into a little room, not much more than a cubbyhole, where the cleaning staff could change their clothes and have their coffee break. They sat down at a small table.

"Would you like some coffee?"

"No, thank you," said Stefan. Judy just shook

her head. Her mind was racing and Mr Balderson's kaleidoscope conversations were suddenly very real to her. All those little fragments. Were they about to sort themselves into a pattern?

The woman sat down opposite them and put both hands palms-down on the little table. They were work-roughened now. Judy saw a chipped nail, and raw scuffed knuckles. But they were small delicate hands and the nails were varnished red. They spoke of a very different life before this one.

"It was I. I sent the letter."

Into the shocked silence William delivered himself of a thought.

"But you can't be Rashid. Rashid is a boy's name. Have you got a boy's name? There are some names like Hilary and Lesley…"

"William." It was Stefan who spoke. "I think we should just listen."

"I will tell you."

"English please," said Judy, for the woman had spoken in Farsi. "These are my friends. I want them to hear too."

275

"My name is Soheila, and I sent it from here. I put it in a letter box only a few days after I got here."

In Judy a hundred questions jostled for attention.

"I don't understand. Why didn't Rashid post it himself?"

"He gave it to me, Rashid. He asked me to post it when I was safe, when I knew that it would be sure to arrive safely. He had some difficulties. He had to be very careful, he said. Only the mountain paths, and the secret ways. For me it was easier – just the long walk, and the waiting, and the walking again. I was just one of many. The letter would be safer with me, and Rashid was sure that when I got here, they would let me stay. "

"How could he know that?"

The woman had been gazing intently into Judy's eyes. "He said when they saw my back they would let me stay. And it was true."

"I don't understand."

"I was at the university, studying law. I was interested in politics. Then I walked with a male student friend; he was not related to me, my hair was showing. It was enough."

She looked up again. Dark eyes met dark eyes. Stefan could almost believe they were related.

"Oh, I see," said Judy. But Stefan didn't.

"It was enough? Enough for what please?"

"For two hundred lashes."

Stefan stood up and frowned. He went red in the face. He said crossly,

"You should not make up stupid stories."

Judy said, "It is true, Stefan, I promise you."

Stefan turned his face to the wall. Something was bubbling up inside him and he didn't want them to see it. He hadn't felt like that before, and he was worried about what would happen if he let it out. If he started breaking furniture or smashing his fist into the window then they would be frightened, and that would make him just another one on the long, long list of people who use fear. If Karl had been there and said something stupid then he would have had something to do, but luckily for Karl he wasn't. Stefan felt his eyes sting.

"So you see your father came here looking for him, just like you," the woman continued. "He was sure that he would be here, because this is where the letter came from. But I couldn't tell him much, except that Rashid never did come here. I met your father at the asylum centre, before I got my residence permit."

"So where did my father go? Where is Rashid?"

"I am sorry, but I cannot answer your questions."

"So." Judy spoke softly, almost to herself. "Rashid and my father could be anywhere."

Judy put her head in her hands, and the woman reached out across the table to take them in her own. Judy let her.

"I am sorry, my dear." The woman said in Farsi. "But even a small piece of the truth is better than the darkness of complete ignorance."

Judy wasn't so sure. Her last chance of finding her father was shot to pieces. But remembering her manners she finally managed to say, "Thank you for your help," before they left the museum and walked back out into the daylight.

"I am going to talk to the head of the museum," said William. "I wonder if you can look him up in the phone book. He will know all about my key and what it opens. There are lots of different kinds of keys, aren't there? There are door keys, and keys to treasure chests, and keys to cars – though it can't be a car key of course, because there were no cars a thousand years ago. Pianos have keys too, but they don't count…"

"William," said Stefan, "you haven't seen my favourite shop yet. You must see it before you leave."

"It doesn't matter so much."

"But it matters to me. You are my workmate. I want to show my workmate."

"All right."

"Judy, go to the café," said Stefan, pointing down the street. "Mr Balderson will be there by now. We will come after soon."

Judy looked gratefully at Stefan. She didn't want to spoil William's great moment, and she really did need a few minutes to herself. She walked down the steps and turned back along the street towards the town square, pulling up the hood of her parka and sticking her hands in her pockets as she walked. A biting easterly wind was getting up, the wind that sometimes strikes the Swedish coast in winter after travelling across the frozen Baltic with neither a hill to break its force nor a drop of open water to relieve its chill.

So her little adventure was at its end. Her fantasy about the great quest, the epic search – whatever she'd told herself this was – it was over. Now she was back in the real world, trudging down the icy streets of a Swedish seaport with the wind in her face and no particular place to go except back to England and into a foster home. Her father could be absolutely anywhere, doing absolutely anything, but the most likely thing was that he had headed back East, trying to pick up Rashid's trail. And then, as she very well knew, anything could have happened.

A man stood on the steps of a little hotel on the outskirts of town. He looked up and down the empty street feeling more hopeful than he had for a long time. His task had turned out to be much, much harder than he expected. Back in England, when he had caught sight of the girl hurrying out of the park gates, it had seemed easy enough. He had followed her and seen her enter the bus station but then, in the evening crowd of travellers, he had lost her. Determination and luck had kept him on her track, and he had almost caught up with her before she left England. Then followed a seemingly hopeless trek across Europe, but there was never any question of giving up. He had a task to complete, a duty to perform, and however unpleasant it was going to be, he was determined to see it through. If he didn't, then his own life would not be worth living. So he had come at last to this little town. He had asked around, and it had been quite easy – English tourists, travelling in a camper van, a tall strange man, two children. The closer he got, the easier it became to get information. After all, everybody knew everybody. Strangers were a rarity to be talked about at length. For the first time for weeks he could relax a bit. They were in the area, somewhere. He would be able to accomplish his terrible task. But it was shockingly cold, he had had no idea; so he had kitted himself out that morning in some second-hand winter clothing from one of the few shops that were open. It was a sort of army surplus store, where you could buy fur hats and boots and snow-gaiters and the like that were no longer standard issue. There were even some collectors' items that were popular with the visitors – winter coats and hats and officers' insignia from the Soviet era that the Russian tourists who now flooded over the border in summer brought with them to sell.

Today, at last, he could do his duty. She couldn't be far away.

Mr Balderson was already in the café, seated at a table in the corner with a large cup of tea and a bilberry muffin in front of him. Judy made her way over and sat down opposite. Looking at him now, Mr Balderson suddenly looked very old – not just an elderly man, but ancient. The lines on his face seemed deeper, the scar where his right eye had been more puckered, his neck thin and wrinkled. He had taken off his hat, and the bald patch on the top of his head looked dry and dull rather than shiny like it had been before. Even his hair looked tired, hanging around his head in sparse wisps. He certainly wasn't a pretty sight, and the almost fingerless hand that rested on the table didn't make him any prettier. But the blue gimlet eye that looked right into her was unchanged.

She told him about the visit to the museum.

"He was here," she finished, "but now he's gone. He must have gone east, months ago, to find out why Rashid never came."

"So," said Mr Balderson, "you have gained knowledge. You understand why he left you alone for so long without a word. A piece of the puzzle, a glimpse of the truth."

"But now—" Judy began.

"Now you fear for him. Knowledge is not always comfortable. But on the whole, necessary, in my view. *'The truth thee shall deliver, it is no dread.'* I've always thought that was rather well said."

As far as Judy could see, all that the truth had delivered so far was a miserable journey back to a foster home and an endless wait for news of her father. She was so not looking forward to that. But that was how it looked.

"It's just a dead end, Mr Balderson, whatever you say."

"Dead end," repeated Mr Balderson. "An odd

expression that would certainly interest William. Is even death itself a dead end? Your journey is only now beginning. You have passed through the valley of the quest, but there are more valleys ahead, and still a long road to travel. For both of us."

He stared at her and took a bite of his muffin.

Judy sighed. Mr Balderson was being very serious, but sometimes his philosophizing was a bit hard to bear, and this was one of those times; she wasn't in the mood for it. She was feeling tired and hopeless and stupid. She shook her head.

"It's no good, Mr Balderson, I don't understand a word of what you are saying."

"But your father would. Oh yes, he would know exactly what I'm talking about."

Stefan and William came in. Stefan was holding forth about the relative merits of silver or copper in peaty water, and the problems they would face if the spring thaw came too quickly.

"I found a pike, once, quite a big one, two and a half kilos perhaps, in the top of a bush thirty metres from the riverbank – there was much spring water that year, much snow in the…"

But William had seen Mr Balderson and started talking before he was half way across the room.

"It's a key! There was one just like in the museum! It's a thousand years old, the cleaning lady told me. It's the oldest thing I've ever found, and it was under the tree. If there hadn't been a storm I would never have found it there."

Mr Balderson smiled, and something lit up his face, smoothing away the years.

"The tree fell, your journey began, and it has ended here. William, you are truly favoured. It is no less than deserved. You have gained knowledge! And so has Judy. Your key was the key!"

"Yes I know my key was a key, I just told you."

Mr Balderson said something under his breath. Judy caught a few words about the gods favouring the innocent. She got the point. And she *was* happy for William.

Meanwhile Stefan was tucking into a huge cream- and marzipan-filled bun that he had fetched for himself, one of two that almost didn't fit on to the plate. Judy wondered briefly how many of them he could eat if he really made the effort. She would have to test him some time. Except that there wouldn't be a "some time".

Stefan looked up at the clock on the wall above their heads.

"I must go to the bus station soon, or I miss the last bus."

Now, suddenly, it was there. Stefan would go back to his farm, Judy and William would – well, Judy didn't really know what they would do, but it was over. It wasn't a very nice feeling. She felt cold, and even lonelier than she had felt in the houseboat on Christmas Eve.

"Are we going home now, Judy?" asked William.

Judy nodded.

"Looks like it, William. We can't stay here for ever, and Mr Balderson…" She looked at him, but he simply smiled, and took another bite of his muffin.

"Why can't you come with us, Stefan?" said William. "You can make Judy laugh. And I'd like it a lot."

"So would I, Stefan," said Judy, taking herself by surprise.

Stefan mumbled something.

"What?" said William.

Stefan wiped cream of his mouth and spoke slightly more clearly.

"I will not like not coming with you. I am not happy to say goodbye."

Mr Balderson stood up.

"I shall return to the camper – I parked it in the square. You will wish to accompany Stefan to the bus station and say your farewells." He picked up his hat and left the café. They watched him stride past the window, his long coat flapping, his head, with its drapery of white hair, perching on a thin neck. For a moment he looked like some huge exotic bird.

Once he had gone, nobody had very much to say. Stefan cleaned the last of the cream off his plate. Judy drank up her tea. They stood up and left. The wind had dropped while they were in the café and it had started to snow, one of those sudden heavy falls of late winter, with flakes the size of chicken feathers, that quickly covers everything in a fresh white coat and is as quickly gone again when the weather makes its next turn. They walked together

287

in silence – even William seemed to have run out of steam – to the corner of the street.

Judy and Stefan looked at each other.

Stefan looked down at the warm boots that Farmor had exchanged for Judy's scuffed trainers a long time ago.

"When can we come back?" William wanted to know. More than anything he wanted very much to go back to the museum and hear more about ancient keys.

"William," said Judy "We may never come back." She couldn't think of a nicer way to put it.

William looked absolutely miserable.

"I can find the name and address of someone who works there," said Stefan. "There is probably a lot on the internet. You can talk to him on the telephone when you get home."

"But when will I get home?"

Neither of them had an answer to that.

Stefan turned to Judy. "And you will write me a letter please? To help me with my English, you know," he added lamely.

"Yes. Will you reply?"

"You know that I will."

Funnily, Judy did know.

Stefan turned away from them. They watched him walk off down the street.

19

Judy and William headed for the square along streets that were now completely empty. The last booted and scarved pedestrians had long ago hurried home to their warm kitchens and evening meals. They arrived at the main square, now lying silent and muffled in snow. The municipal flower beds and benches were just white lumps, and the kiosk that in summer housed the tourist information office was boarded up. In the middle of the lamp-lit square was a tall flagpole. Along one side was space for parking, but the camper wasn't in it.

"Is this the right place?" wondered William aloud.

Judy looked around. "I'm sure of it."

They walked all round the square, checking down side streets just in case, but there was no camper.

"Maybe he's gone to get petrol or something."

There was nowhere to sit. The snowfall stopped as suddenly as it had started, and the wind got up again, making the flagpole's long lanyard snap and slap rhythmically.

"Look, a flag!" said William, not pointing at the flagpole but at a pile of old snow several metres high and now white and fresh like a miniature Himalaya. Planted on the top of it was a small tattered flag. It looked like a miniature version of the prayer flags that adorn the high passes of Tibet. William walked over to the hill of snow and started to climb up it. Judy followed.

"Look, it's the feather."

Tied to the top of the little pole was, unmistakeably, the capercaillie feather they had last seen in Mr Balderson's hat. The flag, when they got closer, turned out to have been made from an old handkerchief. There was writing on it, blurred where the ink had run. Judy took down the flag and made out the words,

"You enter the second valley. Our ways part."

"There's your bag," said William, "and my collection, too." They lay on the other side of the snow-mound, and had been hidden from view.

Mr Balderson had gone.

Stefan was sitting right at the back of the bus, as usual. It was practically empty, and luckily there was no one he knew, because he didn't want to talk to anybody. The driver started the engine, and the bus began to pull away. He heard a shout and looked out to see a head with dark hair flying; too late, the bus was gaining on it. Stefan jumped up and ran forward.

Outside Judy saw the bus, incredibly, slow down again and stop. The door slid open to reveal Stefan, with an enormous grin on his face.

"You run pretty fast. Is William coming?"

"He's a bit behind. Can we wait?"

Stefan said a few words to the driver, who shrugged and nodded. The last bus, a winter night; of course he could wait.

William struggled up after a while. He was no slouch, lean as whippet and surprisingly tough considering his diet of bread and butter and his objection to vegetables, but his collection weighed a lot.

At last they were perched in a row on the back seat, Judy and William still breathless and gasping.

"It is good that you have changed your mind. Farmor will be glad," he said.

"Are you sure?" asked Judy.

"Yes." Stefan paused for moment. "I also."

"But we didn't change our minds," said William. "Mr Balderson went away and left us here. We had to come."

Judy sighed inwardly as she saw Stefan absorb this information. William went on, "But I'm very glad, because I can talk to the man at the museum now and I can tell Farmor about the key and here there's no school."

Stefan turned to William and punched him gently on the shoulder.

"And I still have my workmate."

Judy had been looking for the right words. She

said, "Stefan, I … I didn't really..." She tried again. "There wasn't anything else to do, except go."

"You mean you wished to stay?"

"Yes."

"Then why did you not tell me in the café?"

"How could I? It would have been … after all you've done … presumptuous."

"What is that?" Stefan was smiling.

"Um … forward."

"Forward? So instead you were backward."

"You could say that, I suppose."

"I do say that."

After a while, Stefan said,

"Mr Balderson sees with his soul. He is not backward. He makes you do what you want to do."

It was already late evening when the bus left them outside the village store. It was so late there was no one about. They stood and watched the tail lights get smaller and smaller until Stefan turned to Judy and William, saying, "Come with me, please."

They followed him up a side street and quickly came to the edge of the village proper, where the houses gave way to fields, then turned up a track that led off between granite gateposts and towards a two-storeyed timbered house with a huge old barn attached to the gable-end. In winters past, the inhabitants could walk through and tend to their animals without going out of doors at all. There were several big outhouses – it was almost a little village in itself, and had clearly been the home of farming nobility at one time.

"Stefan, where are we going?"

"I would sleep here tonight, and go home with the postman tomorrow. You will stay here too."

"But—"

"Please do not be backward, Judy. There is plenty of room. It is a big house."

They ascended wooden steps to a wide roofed porch. Above the carved and panelled door was a huge pair of elk antlers. Stefan called out briefly, and – in a way that was now familiar to Judy and William – walked straight in. They followed, and found themselves in a hallway that seemed not to have changed much in the last hundred years, with broad wooden floorboards, half-panelling on the walls, and a tallboy that was the worse for wear. A staircase swept up in an elegant curve to the upper floor, and a door leading off the hall opened, with a boy of about Stefan's age, stocky, with dark hair and long arms, emerging from it. Judy swallowed. It was Karl.

Stefan launched into a speech that for him was pretty long. He spoke – deliberately Judy guessed – in broad dialect. It was practically another language from the simple words she had learnt; she understood nothing. When he was finished, Karl nodded. He turned and led the way up the staircase.

There was an upper hall, with doors leading off it in two directions, and Karl opened one of them and turned on the light. There was nothing much to see. The roof slanted, they were almost under the eaves, and on the floor was a pile of fleeces. There was even, Judy found out later, a bearskin and an extremely old wolfskin rug, which had been thrown over the knees of Karl's great-grandmother when she rode in her trap to church. The room was unheated.

Stefan and Karl stood talking in low voices while William and Judy were making themselves comfortable. Stefan went over to Judy.

"Karl says he is sorry it is not the proper guest room. He can't—"

"It's all right. I know what he thinks about me."

Stefan replied in a low voice that was so hard and fierce that Judy was shocked.

"You do not know. You know nothing. You are my friend, he knows who you are, you are here, you are a guest. He has seen you fight, he has seen you laugh. If you fall down he will pick you up. But his grandfather is an old hard man, with a hard hand, sitting downstairs in the kitchen. Some time you must think how it is to be Karl."

It was true. She had made her mind up on that bridge and done exactly what she blamed others for. Made him one of "them" without knowing anything about him. She walked over to Karl who was standing in the doorway and chewing his lip. She held out her hand and said, in her best Swedish,

"Thank you, we will be very comfortable here."

Stefan was beside her again.

"There is something more Karl said. It is important, I think. Karl says someone was looking for you in the village earlier this evening. Anna told him, she works sometimes in the café."

"Looking for me?" Judy's first thought was that Mr Balderson had returned for some reason. But everybody knew him. He wasn't "somebody". And he knew where she would be.

"He knew your name. He asked about you."

"But it's impossible." Suddenly a wave of mad hope swept over Judy. Had he found her? Had her father somehow, by some miracle, found *her*?

She turned breathlessly to Karl,

"Please tell me, where is he now, what did he look like?"

Stefan translated, listened to Karl's reply.

"He was foreign, speaking English, he had a little car."

Then a wild thought struck her.

"Was it blue? What was the number plate? Was it 377?"

Karl looked apologetic when Stefan translated this. He explained that Anna had not told him so very much. He could ask her tomorrow. But the man had been quite short, and he had a limp.

"Stefan, it's him! It must be. The man who has been following us."

Stefan was totally confused.

"What man? Now we will sit down and you will tell me all about this. He herded both Judy and Karl over to the pile of fleeces, and they sat down. William had already snuggled into the bearskin, but now he sat up. In the dimly lit room they listened as Judy explained about the social worker, and being chased all the way to the docks, and getting away just in time. But it seemed he had chased her all the way to the North of Sweden.

Stefan said,

"In Sweden the social people work very hard, but not this hard."

Karl snorted and said something.

"He says that he is not a social worker. He is probably a kidnapper. Or a murderer, like in the films. But of course not – Karl likes exciting stories," he added hastily, when he saw William's face.

Judy's mind had been racing, trying to fit the pieces together. She remembered her father saying that Rashid was not just anybody, that he might be followed, that there was danger. And there was Soheila, too, at the museum, saying that Rashid had given her the letter for safety's sake. And now her father, disappeared somewhere, looking for Rashid. There was only one logical answer. This man thought that she knew something, that she could somehow lead him to Rashid, or her father, or both. He didn't know that she hadn't heard a single word from either of them. Karl had obviously seen too many action movies, but still… Stefan broke in on her thoughts.

"Well he will find you soon. It is not hard to know where you are."

Thoughts tumbled into Judy's head. She would have to run away again, and this time there was no Mr Balderson to help them. And what about William? And where could she go?

"It is very good," Stefan went on. "We do not have to look for him, he will find us."

"Good, how is it good? I have to get away."

"But we must stop him, of course. We must make *him* go away. Anna says he was quite a small person, and all alone. You told me this too."

"But…"

"Judy this cannot be very hard for you to understand. Are you going to run away all the time? Then you are not that person that I thought: the person who stops, and turns around, and goes to meet the problem. I saw you on the bridge, and so did Anna." He smiled happily at the memory. "But now we do something together. This man you can tip into the river if you wish and I will not be cross. But first we must talk to him."

Judy saw then that Stefan was right. Completely right. It was all so obvious to him; he didn't have to think about it at all. If there was one tiny little clue left about her father, one thing that connected her to him, then it was this man.

"How will we do that?"

"We will sit on him, and push snow up his nose." Stefan laughed happily. "But now we must go, quickly," said Stefan. "He may know already where we are living." There was one thing that Stefan did not take so light-heartedly, and that was the thought of the stranger turning up at the farm in the middle of the night, where Farmor was all alone. Snatching up the wolfskin, Stefan made his way down the stairs and out on to the porch, with Judy and William close behind.

"Wait here please," he said, and he disappeared in the direction of one of the outhouses.

After a while they heard a raucous engine, and a snowmobile roared into view, driven by a helmeted Karl in full winter gear with Stefan, also helmeted, riding pillion. The snowmobile was dragging a high-sided sled. It stopped in front of the porch.

"Get in please, and cover yourselves," called Stefan. Judy and William did as they were told.

The snowmobile shot off at a ridiculous pace, bumping and swaying across snowbound ditches and frozen streams, and although they were no longer in the grip of midwinter temperatures they had to burrow down to get out of the chill wind of their passage. They soon found out that for warmth there is nothing in the whole wide world that beats the pelt of a wolf. In half an hour they were already at the bottom of the farm track. They climbed out. Stefan got off and took off his helmet, throwing it into the sled and saying, "Tack." Then a slight argument followed. It was clear that Karl, having got this far, was not going to miss the fun. Stefan gave in, and all four of them started off up the track.

The light in the farmhouse porch beckoned. The kitchen, the parlour with its tiled stove, Farmor. William wasn't really conscious of it, but he had a warm feeling somewhere in the region of his stomach, which, if he had only known it, was what it feels like when you are coming home. Judy felt safe, oddly enough. They were both, in their different ways, comforted just by being there.

Then they all saw the small car parked in front of the house.

"He's here!" gasped Judy. Stefan was already running up the last bit of track, with Karl at his heels.

"Stefan, wait..." Judy hissed, but Stefan had no time for thinking or planning. If this person had done anything to upset Farmor then he would regret it, and Stefan would see to that personally. He made his way up to the kitchen window in complete silence, and motioned to Karl to go around the back of the house. As he looked in the window, Stefan saw that Farmor was alone in the kitchen, energetically scrubbing the kitchen table. He beckoned to Judy and William, and they crept up to join him. Karl came round the house, shaking his head.

"I can't see him," said Stefan. "Farmor is alone. He could be anywhere. But she must have heard his car, I don't understand. You must stay out of sight, Karl and I will go in."

But Judy wasn't having any of that.

"If he is outside somewhere we will be safer indoors, won't we?" Judy spoke in a low whisper. "We can't just stay out here until he finds us; he might even be watching us now." As soon as she said it, she wished she hadn't – suddenly every shadow had eyes. William was clutching her arm. "If we go in there will be four of us. What can he do?"

Stefan could imagine quite a lot of things, setting the house on fire for starters, but he didn't mention them. Judy was right – he couldn't leave William and her outside in the dark. So they all moved quietly towards the front porch, expecting that at any moment some dark shadow would separate itself from the wall of the woodshed or the barn and spring at them. Judy saw to her horror that Karl had his hand on the hunting knife that hung at his belt, calmly loosening it in its sheath. They reached the door and stepped into the hall, Stefan calling out quickly and loudly to Farmor so as not to frighten her; she came from the kitchen, wiping her hands on her apron.

"Oh, Stefan! And Judy and William, what a lovely surprise. And Karl too—"

Stefan interrupted her with a hail of questions, and she calmed him as best she could.

"Stefan, I am perfectly all right, I am well. But where is Mr Balderson? I didn't hear the van coming."

But there was something in the way that Farmor spoke that made them take notice. She was just a bit too cheerful.

"Farmor..."

"Stefan – all of you – come into the kitchen, please. No, Stefan," she said, as he tried again to find out what was going on. "In the kitchen. Then I will explain."

Farmor was definitely on edge. She smoothed down her apron and kept touching her grey hair. They trooped into the kitchen.

"Please, Farmor," said Stefan. "Is the man here or not? We have to know. He might be dangerous."

This seemed to cheer Farmor up considerably.

"You don't say! Oh good, that is good," she said as she beamed at her grandson.

Then Farmor took a deep breath.

"I was resting in the living-room, very tired after blacking the stove, and I fell asleep. I was woken up by the car, and I saw him get out and look around, then he came towards the house. I saw him clearly, so I had some time to think. He called out – it wasn't Swedish, it wasn't English – so I knew. Then he opened the door and stood there. It was easy, I was ready."

"Ready, Farmor? Ready for what?"

"I shot him, of course."

20

Farmor's words didn't have the effect she had been hoping for. She hadn't been expecting applause or backslapping exactly, but something on the lines of "Well done, Farmor, didn't know you had it in you" would have been nice. Instead she was met by silence, and wide-eyed, opened-mouth faces that looked at her as though she had just landed from outer space. Karl found his voice first, the only one of them who seemed impressed, uttering the Swedish equivalent of "wow". Then Judy and Stefan spoke almost in unison,

"You SHOT him?"

"As I said, I shot the Russian. I didn't have the elk-gun, it's locked away and there wasn't time, but the shotgun was in the kitchen for the magpies – only birdshot, but it had to do. My grandfather would be proud of me," she ended firmly, and she stuck out her bottom lip stubbornly, suddenly five years old again.

Stefan and Judy were speechless, but William wasn't.

"Is he dead? Where's the body? Did you bury it?"

Farmor felt that Stefan was not as pleased as she was, and Judy was white as sheet. But of course, they had been brought up in peaceful times. They knew nothing of what she had lived through. She spoke to William.

"No, William, he is not dead. He was breathing and moaning when I last looked."

"Where is he?"

"In the root cellar. It has a good door, and I've put a poker through the latch just to be sure."

"How do you know he's Russian?" asked Judy.

"Judy, dear, I *saw* him. That long grey coat, the hat, fur-lined, with the ear-flaps, and the little red star on the front – and the bad footwear; they were always badly equipped, you know. I was only a child, but I never forgot. Now I am not a child, now I have done something to help you. When the Russians are after you, you must have help."

Farmor had come to care for Judy a lot. She had cried a bit when she left. It wasn't just that she had done so much for Stefan – changed his life, actually – it was also that Farmor had never had a daughter or a granddaughter, and Judy reminded her a bit of herself at that age. So if something that had troubled the girl had been got out of the way, then Farmor was glad. And if that something was Russian, so much the better. But now it was time to get things neat and tidy again.

So armed with a couple of torches they set off for the root cellar. There wasn't much to see as they approached it, only a mound of snow to one side of the barn, but as they got closer Judy saw the stone steps leading downwards to a small wooden door. The cellar was vaulted, below ground, and built entirely of well-fitted blocks of granite. It could have been the crypt of a mediaeval church, or an Etruscan tomb. Even in the depths of winter it kept a constant temperature just above freezing, and it was correspondingly cool and dark on the hottest summer day. Stefan went down first to remove Farmor's poker from the latch and open the door. Inside there was a small space and then another door that was also set in stone doorposts. Carefully he opened the second door; a faint light glowed inside. Farmor had placed a candle on the sandy floor – just enough to raise the temperature a few degrees without putting her cabbages at risk. Shelves along the walls held jars and bottles, all neatly labelled with contents and date – bilberry, wortleberry, wild raspberry, garden raspberry, cloudberry, blackcurrant. One shelf was for the precious red cabbages, carefully positioned so as not to touch each other. Hemp sacks on the floor held potatoes, carrots, beets. And, lying on his back with his head supported by a half-empty sack of parsnips, was the man who had come all the way from England to find them. They could indeed have been back in the world of Farmor's childhood, or even, thought Judy as she ducked under the lintel and followed Karl into the cellar, the First World War, in some dugout in the trenches of Flanders –

the weak guttering candlelight, the figure lying in his greatcoat, sleeping, wounded, or dead. William crowded in after them, but Farmor waited outside. She had a firm grip on the old double-barrelled shotgun, prepared for any breakout attempt on the part of the wily Russian.

"Is he still alive?" she called.

Stefan moved closer and shone his torch on the face of the prone figure. He heard fast shallow breathing, as the man's eyelids fluttered in the torchlight.

"Yes, he's alive." Stefan bent down to feel the man's forehead; in the cold damp air of the cellar it was a surprise to find that he was hot. "He won't last much longer down here," Stefan added, looking at the shot-riddled right shoulder of the greatcoat and the dark clotted blood.

"Well, I can't have a Russian in the house. It'll have to be the sauna."

The man parted his dry, cracked lips and tried to wet them with his tongue. His jaw, covered in dark stubble, moved slowly as he spoke. It was barely a whisper.

Judy caught only a single word, but that was enough. "*Ab*," he croaked. Water. "He's not Russian, Farmor," she called.

It was a lot easier to get him out of the cellar than it had been for Farmor to get him in all on her own. Stefan and Karl fetched the tailgate from one of the old farm wagons, manoeuvred him on to it, and carried him back to the house. Then they said goodbye to Karl, who was a bit disappointed about having missed the best bit but still felt he'd had a good outing. The wounded man was soon ensconced in the kitchen settle, his greatcoat carefully removed and his shirt cut off with the kitchen scissors so that Farmor could study the damage. She wasn't exactly feeling guilty. Accidents will happen with shotguns, and even if he wasn't Russian he *had* been following Judy and *might* have been planning something very nasty. But for now he was helpless, and she felt that the thing to do was get him cleaned up. As they removed his outer clothing and got a better look at him, it was hard to believe that he could be dangerous. There were no concealed weapons, Stefan had made very sure of that.

Judy and William were sent out of the kitchen while Stefan and Farmor got to work with the tweezers, removing birdshot from his shoulder and upper chest. Stefan held him still, while Farmor in her reading glasses poked carefully around, finding the small lead pellets and dropping them with a little plinging noise into a tooth glass. There were some moans, and once he cried out, but whoever he was he seemed to be no stranger to pain; Farmor remembered once removing birdshot from her husband's left buttock, and he had made a lot more fuss. Farmor even found that she was starting to warm to the man, not only because of his stoicism, the old scars on his chest and arms, and his thin weak body, but because it is just very difficult to dislike someone whose wounds you have tended, and whose suffering you have eased. Perhaps that's why it's a good idea to do it. Anyway, when they were done poking about he got a good dollop of her very special ointment, and a clean neat bandage. When Judy and William came back into the kitchen

Farmor was carefully dribbling thin gruel into the man's mouth with a teaspoon.

"He should sleep now. And so must we. Tomorrow we will ask some questions."

"But what if he wakes up, and just leaves in the middle of the night?"

"I don't think he will wake up."

"And even if he does," said Stefan, entering the kitchen from the hall and holding up a handful of cables and a distributor cap, "he won't get far."

They went to bed, leaving the stranger well tucked in and breathing quietly.

Judy lay on the parlour sofa under her duvet. She was exhausted, but her head was far too full of thoughts and questions for sleep. It was all she could do not to get up again and go to the kitchen and shake the wounded man until he spoke. At least the boot was firmly on the other foot now. From the hunter to the hunted – he was in their power thanks to Farmor and her shotgun, and tomorrow there would be answers, it was no good worrying at it now like a puppy with a slipper. And yet ... now that she had actually seen him, with his thin face and skinny arms, he just didn't seem to be equipped for a kidnapping. He was very determined, anyway, doggedly following her all the way here.

Judy heard the parlour door open in the darkness.

"William?" He wasn't much of a sleeper, and sometimes he had very important questions to ask in the middle of the night. She had never been able to get into his head that some things could wait until morning. She reached out and found the switch of the standard lamp. Standing just inside the room, clutching at the door frame to keep himself upright, stood the wounded stranger, his face a pale mask, the half-grown beard a black shadow, the eyes staring at her, in some form of delirium.

"Judy Azad."

"What do you want? Keep away from me."

She opened her mouth to yell and bring Stefan and Farmor running.

"Please, I beg of you, I must talk to you alone."

Well, this *was* what she had wanted. She could always yell later, if it turned out to be necessary. Right now he looked as though a faint breeze would blow him over. She threw her duvet aside and stood up as the man let go of the door frame and staggered to the sofa. Slumping on to it, he leant back for a few moments with closed eyes, then gathered himself again, and looked up at her.

"My name is Rashid. I am your father's friend."

"No you're not." He couldn't be. Rashid had never made it to Europe. This man clearly had no idea of her meeting with Soheila; he didn't know that she knew. This was some kind of trick, but it had failed. "I am Rashid," he said again. "Your father… He told me to say something to you."

Judy said nothing.

"He told me to say, 'Only two cupcakes.'"

Judy closed her eyes.

She was back in the houseboat on a rainy Sunday evening. It was her father's birthday, and she had prepared a surprise for him. The little stove was lit, and the rain pattered quietly on the roof. She had made cupcakes, a whole tray full of them, icing letters on each one so that they spelled his name, and her father was overwhelmed. He had given her a huge hug and danced a little dance, bumping his head on the overhead locker as usual, and had said that he was going to eat at least ten cupcakes. She had given him two. He pretended to be deeply hurt, and complained that she was starving him, on his own birthday. She replied, "But I'm counting in binary code – I gave you ten." It was the kind of joke that he loved. He was like that; he had chuckled about it for days.

Only her father could have known what those words would mean to her.

"Where is my father? Where is he? Why is he not with you?"

Rashid had tried to prepare himself for this moment. There had hardly been an hour of the day, or a sleepless night, when he hadn't thought about this meeting; how to get it right. But there is no way to get such a thing right; he knew that now. He looked at the girl facing him. She had his best friend's eyes, the same high cheekbones and determined look.

"He came to help me, Judy…"

His eyes overflowed and he buried his face in his hands.

"I am so sorry. He is dead."

21

Farmor knew a thing or two about despair, mourning and sorrow. They are like a disease. Not a romantic disease, if there is such a thing: flowers at the bedside, kind nurses, quiet voices. More like lung cancer or leprosy – an ugly disease. Even the kindest people sometimes find it hard to be with the open wounds, the anger. Some people, struck down by sorrow, are like needy puppies, seeking attention, wanting to draw others in and make them a part of it, unable to be alone, talking, talking, talking. Others are cats. You have to search all over the place for an injured cat. It hides away, as only a cat can hide, out of reach, under floorboards, at the back of cupboards, among tree-roots at the bottom of the garden, trying to absorb its pain into itself, waiting in silence and the dark for the wounds to scar over, or for death to come and fetch it.

Judy was a cat; Farmor was quite clear about that.

Stefan found her the next day, sitting in the corner of an old round-timbered hay-store a couple of kilometres from the farm; it lay dilapidated and half-sunk on the edge of marshland that was now frozen and silent.

A fresh fall of powder snow had covered her tracks, but Silla led Stefan to the little hut. As he approached in the slanting morning light he saw Judy's skis and sticks leaning against the wall by the low entrance. He pushed opened a rickety door of rough planks and ducked inside. A couple of months ago she would have been in a very bad way after a night outdoors, but already the world had turned towards the promise of Spring, and so the night had been tolerable. Silla bounded in, and threw herself at the small figure huddling in the corner, half-covered in old dust-grey hay. Silla tried to lick her face, but got pushed away, so she lay down and whined softly, her tail waving gently.

Stefan was carrying a rucksack. He shrugged it off and started wordlessly to unpack it. Farmor had been thorough. There was a sleeping bag, a thermos flask, a bottle of water, a packet of sandwiches and a torch. Judy watched him, dreading the words that he would have to say and that she would have to listen to: *Your father, how terrible, poor you...*

But she was wrong.

"We will have good weather now for a while. If you need help, send Silla. Say 'Go home.' But in Swedish, of course." he said, before turning to Silla to say, "Stay."

And then he left her.

Farmor was well aware that all they could do for Judy was get food into her somehow and wait; that for cat people the weakness and helplessness of mourning means a loss of dignity and integrity that is almost impossible to bear. They need to keep their souls to themselves. But Rashid was another matter. He definitely did not want to have his soul to himself. After weeks and months alone, grimly determined to bring the terrible news to his friend's daughter, he now seemed unable to stop talking. He desperately wanted to tell Judy everything, now that he could. About how her father had made him promise that if anything happened to him he would seek her out, care for her as though she was his own daughter. How he had sworn to do it, or die in the attempt. How he had comforted himself by making plans for their future together, for he had no children of his own. But she wasn't there to talk to, and Farmor had absolutely forbidden him to go to her. So he sat at the kitchen table, drinking coffee and talking to Farmor instead.

Farmor did what she could, nodding sympathetically and reassuring him when for the hundredth time he said,

"What could I have done? There was nothing I could do. And he said to me, again and again, 'Only one thing matters, Rashid. Find my beloved girl, and care for her.'"

But even Farmor, whom life had taught so much – too much – began to tire. She felt old and the strength she did have was for the sad girl hiding out at the bottom of the old hay field. Farmor knew she could heal Rashid's physical wounds, and was more than willing to do so. But she was fairly sure that Judy would stay out of sight as long as Rashid was in the house. If he wanted to heal his soul, Rashid would have to go elsewhere.

It was Stefan who realized what he needed to do, and one morning led Rashid – still weak and with a very stiff shoulder – to the car.

When they arrived at the museum, the hesitant look in Soheila's face, the surprise in Rashid's, the sudden burst of excited talk in a language of which Stefan understood nothing – all of this told him that he had done the right thing.

Judy needed time, and now that Rashid had someone to lean on he would hopefully allow her that.

But while Rashid's life had taken a positive turn, Stefan's life had gone pear-shaped, as Judy would say. His friend was lost, wandering through grief's dark maze, and he couldn't follow her. Sorrow and loneliness are partners in crime – never separated, always together. There was nothing he could say, certainly nothing in his useless English. Even at the best of times he wasn't good at talking. He was better at doing. He tried to think of something he could make for her, or show her, but nothing could have made the slightest dent in her armour, he knew that much.

William also had his cross to bear. Now that he knew that his find was a key he was desperate to know more about it, and talk to someone who knew. He couldn't talk to Mr Balderson, because he had disappeared. Mr Greaves was in England, and if he had known that Stefan was going into town with Rashid he could have gone with them and tried to find someone at the museum, but he hadn't known, or at least not until they had left.

But one thing was good. The sun had some warmth now, and during the day the snowdrifts shrank, and the snow became heavy and wet. At midday meltwater dripped from the roofs, and long icicles formed – dangerously long, like spears, so that he and Stefan had to break them off from the eaves of the barn with long poles so that they wouldn't break off by themselves and impale Farmor when she was on her way to the root cellar. But the thing that really made life easier for William was that in the morning the cold of the night had frozen the surface of the snow to a hard crust that you could walk about on, at least for a few hours. He had never been able to master the skiing thing. It just wouldn't work – the points crossed over themselves, the sticks ended up between his legs, and every twenty yards of so he fell over. But now, until about noon when the crust melted and he was plunged into soaking snow up to his knees, he could wander about as though he were on a city street or a football pitch. It's hard to explain what a nice feeling that is after months of being confined to ploughed roads or skis that you can't even use.

So when Farmor asked him to go down to Judy with some fresh sandwiches, he was happy to do it. He hadn't talked to her at all since she got her news. He ran part of the way, it was so nice to just stretch his legs and lope over the sunlit white fields as though he weighed nothing at all. When he came into the hut he found Judy lying on her back in her sleeping bag with her hands behind her head. Silla lay curled up beside her. They were both stripy, because some of the timbers of the hut were warped, and shafts of sunlight got through and made bright lines across them. Judy looked a bit dangerous when she sat up and turned her eyes towards him – if she had had a tail, she could have been a tiger.

"Farmor said to give you these. Can I have one? I'm quite hungry."

"Of course you can, William," said Judy. At least he'd made her smile, although he hadn't meant to.

"I know you are sad about your father," said William, with his mouth full of sandwich. "Are we going to go home soon? I mean, we found Rashid, though he's gone now. Now we know everything, don't we?"

"William, why should I go *anywhere*? My dad's dead."

It wasn't hard to say the words. She had said them aloud to herself all through the first long night. To get used to them. To train herself.

"Do you remember when you said you wanted to be more like me?" said William, "In the campsite? Well, now you are, aren't you? My dad's dead too. Except he didn't get killed in the desert being a hero, like yours. He killed himself with drugs and things. That's what mum told me. I'm not sad at all, though, so I suppose we aren't really the same."

Judy looked at William, as he looked back at her. She had nice smooth skin and dark hair, but William thought that her eyes looked about a hundred years old, maybe even a thousand. And then Judy's face seemed to sort of fall apart and go all ugly and soft, and a funny noise came out of her throat, and tears started pouring down her face, and she sniffed and gulped as though she had a terrible cold.

William ran away.

He burst into the kitchen and, hopping from one leg to the other, he gabbled at Farmor.

"I've been bad, I'm a bad person, I made Judy unhappy. She was all right before, I didn't mean to, I said something wrong...."

"William, William. What is the matter with Judy?"

"She's crying and crying and crying – a horrible big cry and she won't stop."

"William, come here."

William came towards her with such sadness on his face that Farmor reached out her arms and hugged him. He didn't mind too much, and she smelled quite nice – mostly of cinnamon.

"William, it was you of course who could do this. I love you."

William was quite surprised. No one had ever said that to him before, as far as he could remember. He liked it.

"Do you? But Judy…"

"You will see, William, you will see. Now she can begin." Farmor turned back to her cooking.

"I think I shall make a call to Jonas," she said to herself.

Judy showed up in the kitchen that evening with Silla at her heels, announcing that there was no reason to run backwards and forwards with stuff, but she was very grateful for having been given a bit of time to herself.

Over the evening meal, William asked Judy if she had finished crying now.

"Not quite, William," Judy replied quite calmly. "There's probably more where that came from."

"Soon we will have to think about what happens next," said Farmor. "But not yet. Meanwhile I have a little problem. Jonas has got work in Stockholm on the new bypass. I have foolishly promised to look after Matilda, but I am going to need help."

Stefan was surprised. His uncle Jonas was famous for saying that he would rather go out into the woodshed and shoot himself than go south to work. But he said nothing. Sometimes it was better that way with Farmor.

Matilda was a goat, and Stefan went over with a trailer the next morning to pick her up. They got her installed in one of the old loose boxes, though she was far from easy to persuade. She wasn't obstinate so much as curious, and seemed to be starving hungry all the time. William said hello to her, but she started eating the sleeve of his jumper, and then butted him playfully so that he sat down in the muddy slush of the yard. After that he preferred to have nothing to do with her. They finally found out that the easiest way to control her was with ginger biscuits, which she could not resist. Judy held one out, and Matilda followed her meekly into the barn.

Farmor told Judy that she was very sorry to have to ask this of her, when she had such a weight on her soul, but Stefan had school, Farmor herself was simply too busy, and William... Matilda would have to be Judy's sole responsibility. And she was pregnant. Judy said that she didn't mind, as long as Farmor realized that she knew absolutely nothing about goats.

"The thing about animals is just to care," said Farmor. "The rest will follow."

So Judy, having nothing else to do and being quite incapable of reading, and totally unable to solve even the simplest of Stefan's homework problems because everything to do with maths reminded her of her father and brought the tears flooding back, cared for Matilda. She had to be fed, and watered, and mucked out, and she had many different ideas about how to get out of where she was and go somewhere else, so she needed to go for walks and get some fresh air sometimes; Judy had quite a lot to do. Matilda's coat was light golden brown, shading into white on her legs, which were slim and ended in delicate hooves. Her horns curved back from her brow, with an elegant little twist to them that made her look somehow special, like something from a rocky Abyssinian mountainside, rather than a simple domesticated animal. She liked to be scratched behind the ears almost as much as she liked ginger biscuits. But the thing you noticed about her was her eyes. They were golden-green, with a dark oblong pupil. You can't look into a goat's eyes; a goat looks out of its eyes at the world, but it keeps itself to itself. Spaniels, for example, not to mention pigs, have eyes that invite you in, almost begging you to understand what is going on in there, but a goat doesn't ask for anything like that – no sympathy, no understanding, no help. Maybe that's why Judy found that she could talk to Matilda. She talked when they were on their walks, with Matilda on a lead and a pocketful of biscuits to keep her going in a reasonably straight line; and she talked sometimes in the evening, when she had changed the bedding-straw and could sit in the loose-box with her back against warm goat. Matilda never answered, or showed much interest in Judy's remarks. She was more interested in whether there was anything left in her pockets, or seeing if her hair was edible.

Sometimes Judy said things like, "He preferred death with his friend to life with me, didn't he, Matilda? That's simple fact. You think you matter most of all, but you don't – his friendship mattered more, being a hero mattered more, being the kind of person he thought he should be, a story-book person. In his whole life he never broke a promise to anyone, except once – the promise he made to me. He promised to come back, and instead he died. All that stuff about the ties of love, being bound to others, not being free. All that stuff about freedom not being all it's cracked up to be. Well the ties weren't enough to bind him. He broke free and left me."

Sometimes she looked into the future, and saw nothing good about it.

"So, Matilda, what happens now? Nowhere to go

except back to England, a foster-home, a nothing life. I'm not sure I can be bothered. It's a pity Stefan heard that home-made bomb go off. It wasn't so hard just to go to sleep, much easier than I thought it would be. But I'll wait until you've had your kid, anyway. Then I'll decide."

Sometimes she was furiously angry, sometimes she was cool and sensible, trying to think things through, sometimes she laid her cheek against Matilda's flank and wept and cried for her father like a small child in the night. But he didn't answer.

22

It was almost three weeks since Judy found out she was an orphan. On her way back from the barn she stood for a moment in the yard gazing at the sky. It was a starry night, with only a few degrees of frost, and above the northern horizon was an other-worldly greenish glow, that became stronger, shooting up vertical shafts of light. Then the spears and pillars of light seemed to be breathed on by a gentle cosmic breeze. They started moving in waves, billowing like a lacy curtain before an open window, and changing colour, red, then green again, and then purple, until a great curving curtain of dancing light stretched right across the sky, reaching up towards the zenith, high above the forested hills. They had seen the Northern Lights a couple of times since they arrived, but never like this. It was like a visit from outer space – or from outside the universe – that had nothing to do with this earth at all, this tiny little planet that happened to have some people on it, many of them not particularly happy.

"What am I supposed to do, Dad? What shall I do?" asked Judy for the thousandth time. But this time she got an answer. It wasn't like a dream, or a ghost, just a quiet voice speaking inside her head in her father's normal precise voice, reminding her that as she very well knew there was a lot that was wrong with the world, and that some people just had to spend their lives trying to put it right. It felt like they never quite succeeded, and there was never any end to it. It wasn't like making a chair and then sitting on it, or making a cupcake and then eating it, and it certainly wasn't like solving an equation. It was more like gardening. You went on and on, pulling up weeds and watering and pruning, but if you stopped, then the garden would become overgrown.

So if you have nothing else to do, Judy, no love to tie you down, you can be a gardener and weed the world. It is definitely preferable, in my view, to being a goat.

Freedom. She was free, and it was just as awful and lonely as her father had told her it was, ages ago.

The next morning when Judy stepped outside on her way to see to Matilda she found Stefan in the yard carefully waxing two pairs of skis, and humming to himself. He looked up as she approached.

"Ah, you are awake at last."

"It's half past six."

"Yes. But now you are here. Today I think we must go out. I must look at some trees, and you must come with me." He pushed his lower jaw forward and tried to look as if he was in charge. But it didn't last very long. "Please," he added, spoiling the effect.

Judy gazed at him thoughtfully.

"Sure, I'll just get Matilda fed."

There was a special place not far from the farm. A few kilometres away a little hill rose out of flat marshland, a sort of spur that stuck out from the ridge beyond. It was thickly wooded on the lower

335

slopes, but the forest thinned out among great tumbled boulders further up, and if you scrambled right to the top you could get a proper view over the valley and all the way to the village. There were plenty of stories about the trolls and wood-spirits of the place, and there was a spring which never froze – at least that's what people said, though whether anybody had been up there in the depths of winter to check it out was another matter. Stefan and Judy set out early while the snow still bore. Stefan was fairly sure that a she-bear had spent the winter on top of the hill somewhere, and it was getting to the time when she would be waking up and poking her nose out of her den. She might have cubs, so on Farmor's insistence he took a gun. If the worst came to the worst, and she was awake and hungry, and they got between her and her cubs, he might have to use it. But he wasn't like Karl, a hunter at heart. To shoot a bear … it would have to maul Judy or something before he could bring himself to do it.

They set off at a furious pace straight across the open land behind the farm where the snow cover was still good. Stefan realized that Judy had become appallingly quick and apparently tireless, and set out to put her in her place. They skied side by side across the still-frozen snow. Stefan was soon red-faced and sweating while Judy, with a smooth harmonious motion that propelled her yards with every stride, seemed unaffected. The land sloped slightly and then suddenly tipped steeply down towards the marsh. Stefan saw his chance. Downhill his extra weight and greater experience would count in his favour. He planted both his sticks and with a mighty heave he shot off downhill, with Judy, he noticed to his satisfaction, already lagging behind. He tucked his sticks under his arms, went into a skier's crouch, and gained even more speed. Quite close to the bottom of the hill, where the terrain flattened out on to the marsh itself, the snow had settled enough for some small wiry juniper branches to poke up above the surface. The tip of one of Stefan's skis went under one of them instead of over. A mad circus number followed, a cartwheel of arms and legs and skis and sticks, and Stefan went down in a great tangled pile half-buried in the snow. Judy shot past, came neatly to a halt, and scissored back up the slope to where Stefan was trying to sort himself out. It wasn't easy, because without skis he broke through the crust at every step and sank to his knees, swearing.

Judy leant on her sticks and looked down at him.

"Do you need a hand?"

"No, I do not need a hand. I have two hands, as you see."

Judy studied his red face, his injured pride, his attempt to remain serious that was already fighting a losing battle against his usual wide grin, and she laughed.

Stefan heard it – a proper laugh, the first one – and it occurred to him that he should make a complete idiot of himself more often. Why hadn't he thought of that?

They went on, across the marsh and into the forest. The trees there were huge, and the whole place had a primeval air about it. There was old and new growth. Some dry trees were still standing, their bark peeling off in strips, their trunks riddled with small holes where the woodpeckers jammed pine cones to work on the seeds. There was a lot of fallen timber, too, some stretched out on the ground with its roots in the air, some of it caught by its neighbours, and leaning at crazy angles.

They took off their skis – in under the trees the snow was less than a foot deep now, and around the trunks of the bigger ones were patches of bare ground. They scrambled upwards among huge boulders and over rotting trunks, and finally reached the top. Perched on a great boulder almost at the summit they could see out at last – they were level with the very tops of the highest trees. They had a view – and a view is something precious to forest-dwellers. They could make out the roofs of the farm and even, far away, the spiked dome of the church bell-tower in the village.

"What a great place," said Judy. "Is this your land?"

"Not much longer. This may be the last time I come here. We must sell, at least the timber on the root, perhaps even the land. But that is not so different, really."

"Is there no way…?"

"Perhaps if I win on the lottery," said Stefan, and went on. "It is Farmor's best place, with the berries and the mushrooms. Here the flowers come first in the spring, the … they are blue, very blue, and quite small. In the south they are forbidden to pick. But here there are thousands, in among the trees, as soon as the ground is bare. Here we are very careful. We take a tree sometimes, from the north side. Window-wood."

"Window-wood?"

"Yes, it grows very slowly, maybe one hundred years or more, very … tight, hard, you understand. For window frames you must have wood that will not rot. Windows get wet, you know."

Judy was about to say that yes, she did know that, but she changed her mind. She knew nothing, really.

"Here there is no wood for toilet paper and cigarette packets, only real wood," Stefan went on. "Now you must grow timber in sixty years and clear-fell, to make your money. Next spring this is gone, and then I think Farmor will die." He spoke quite matter-of-factly. Then he stood up and said,

"Over there is the spring that never freezes, we should go and see if it is true." He pointed to his left, down the hill. "You can see where it is, next to Stubby Pete."

"Stubby Pete?"

"An old old tree, perhaps the oldest. And a different kind from the others – a pine tree from Spain…" Stefan spoke distractedly, and as Judy drew breath to ask what a tree from Spain was doing on a Swedish hillside, he went on. "But where is he? I can't see him. Come."

He scrambled down, and Judy followed. As they threaded their way down a steep incline between the trees and boulders, Stefan explained.

"There were pilgrims, you see. They walked all the way from the tomb of Jacob in Santiago, to the tomb of Saint Olof in Norway. They passed this way, and had pine cones with them. But no one knows how Stubby Pete came here. A bird, perhaps. But look, I thought so. Stubby Pete is down." They emerged on to a small level place, overhung on the uphill side by an enormous granite block. Sure enough, at its foot was a small mossy-edged pool of dark water. But Stefan was standing contemplating a mass of tangled root as high as man, and a long, twisted trunk that stretched away among the trees below them, its top lost in the undergrowth.

"I must tell Farmor. He didn't want to be here when the machines come, just like her. He must have gone in the big autumn storm. Nobody has been here since then." Stefan turned round to see Judy crouching down over the hole that Stubby Pete's roots had left. There was old snow and ice in there, but the hole wasn't especially deep.

"Stefan, we've got something here for William, I think. He'll be pleased."

Something sharp was sticking up from the gritty half-melted snow. They dug round it and managed to prise loose a small box. They cleaned it up, rubbing it with their mittened hands, scraping off ice and dirt.

"It can't be very old," said Judy. "It should have rusted away long ago. It's made of some metal."

"Maybe it is old," said Stefan. He had been kicking at the snow round the place where the box had lain. "It was underneath something else. He bent down and picked up what looked like a torn piece of old cardboard, and weighed it in his hand. "And if the wood was good…"

"Window-wood."

"Yes, or more likely larch. It lasts for ever."

Judy stowed the box in the front pocket of her windcheater.

When they arrived home, exhausted but well content, the last sunlight was reddening the pine-tops and Judy had made a decision. She had to meet Rashid. He had to be thanked for his efforts, and he had to be told very firmly that there was no possible way she was going to have some kind of adopted stepfather looking after her, however kind he was. She was going to make her own way. Farmor was all in favour of the plan, because Rashid was a problem that had been weighing on her mind. William was over the moon.

"We have to go to the museum to find him, don't we? We can ask about the key, can't we?"

Both Stefan and Judy promised faithfully that this time they would do some proper key research, and not stop until they had got William his answers. They were acutely aware that William had been left pretty much to himself for some time, and it was only fair.

They took the bus from the village, and during the journey to town saw a landscape beginning to change. The roads were clear, the snow-banks on either side shrunken and dirty. Around the boles of the bigger trees, patches of bare ground were visible. You could even imagine that the crowns of the birches had taken on a faint purplish colour, a first tiny hint that at some time – not yet, of course, not yet – the sap would start to rise, and life begin again. In the town itself, people walked at a more relaxed pace, backs seemed straighter, faces more open. Somewhere at the back of everybody's mind a little thought was growing – King Winter might fight a fierce rearguard action, but he was going to lose in the end. They weren't going to say it out loud yet, just in case – a change in the weather could bring two feet of late snow tomorrow, couldn't it? Nevertheless… They entered the museum to find Soheila sitting over her morning coffee in her little room. She jumped up, uncertain at first about how to greet Judy, but saw quickly that she was ready to talk. Rashid was at home in the apartment, she said. They were going to try to get a residence permit for him; it wasn't easy, but they had plans. Did Judy think she could talk to him? When Judy said yes, that was why she had come, they agreed to go to the apartment and meet Rashid. Stefan and William would stay at the museum and start the research.

Soheila pointed them towards a door with a little sign on it saying "Museum staff only" and they went up to it and knocked. It was answered by a young man with a sharp nose and round glasses, who greeted them in a friendly enough way, though it was obvious that he didn't really want to be bothered. That all changed when William reached inside his shirt and pulled out his find. Soon they were inside the room, with the young man sitting at his desk turning William's find over and over in his hands, while they watched in silence, at least for a while. William was about to burst into a flurry of questions, but the young man spoke first.

"Provenance, please?" He spoke perfect English, but that didn't help Stefan or William very much.

"Er..."

"Where did you find it?" The man looked stern. "It is not legal to remove objects from archaeological sites. And without provenance, we are helpless."

"I found it under a tree."

"But where exactly? North of the river, I suppose."

"No, by the canal. In England."

The young man became confused.

"But this is Scandinavian, and probably local work… Of course, it's not impossible, even though it would be remarkable. But in the north part of England, I suppose, not far from the east coast, perhaps?"

"Yes, how did you know?"

"There was a lot of coming and going between Scandinavia and England at the time this artefact would have been made. The north of England was a Scandinavian kingdom almost until the Norman Conquest. Stamford Bridge … but you know of course. You are English."

William did not in fact know, and Stefan certainly didn't, but they didn't mention it.

"I can well imagine that a tradesman or a warrior would wish to keep the key by him. And it is in remarkably good condition, considering."

"Those scratches all along it weren't me. It was like that when I found it."

The young man smiled his first really kind smile at William.

"Those aren't scratches, they are runes. Letters. Now the fun begins." He took a magnifying glass from the desk drawer and began studying the marks carefully while writing on a piece of paper, and then peering again. After a while he leaned back in his chair.

"I don't want to be hasty, but this might be very interesting indeed. Could I borrow it for a while? I would like to consult my colleague and check some things out."

Stefan looked at William and raised a questioning eyebrow.

"It's your find, William."

"Can I have it back later?"

"Of course."

"And will you tell me what it says?"

"I will tell you everything I can."

Stefan kept William occupied with hot chocolate

and a visit to the tackle shop for as long as he could, but he had to take him back in the end. William burst into the museum office without knocking.

The young man had been joined by a much older colleague with a grey beard, and they sat on opposite sides of the desk with William's key between them, engaged in a friendly but very heated debate.

The older man got up and held out his hand when he saw William.

"How do you do? It is you whom we have to thank, I gather, for this little headache," he said, pointing at the find lying on the desk.

"Headache? It didn't give me a headache."

The man looked a bit surprised, but answered cheerfully.

"A nice headache, I assure you, because there are indeed runes engraved on the shaft. Runes are the greatest pleasure for an archaeologist, because they are a form of writing. They are from the period that Erik suggested, before the millennium; well before in my view, though Erik disagrees. One would expect a name, or possibly a charm of some kind, but this is not the case. As far as we can make out, the inscription reads 'böls mun alls batna'."

Now it was William's turn to be confused. "I don't understand."

"No, indeed, it is Old Norse, and means 'All ills grow better'."

The man looked expectantly from William to Stefan and back again. The excited response he expected was obviously not going to happen. He sighed.

"It is a quotation from the *Poetic Edda*, the *Völuspa*, a half-line from the sixty-second stanza. This makes it very important indeed. Because whoever scratched those runes into the shaft must have known the poem, mustn't they? And scholars have been fighting about the date of composition for ages. So if this key can be dated..." Now the younger archaeologist, Erik, broke in.

"I believe it can, if we make contact with your local experts back in England. Did you say you found it under a tree? What do you mean?" William explained about the great storm, and when he mentioned that the tree was an ash, both archaeologists exchanged looks.

"Well, well, it's quite a story. This key may have travelled all over the Nordic lands. It may have been to Iceland, or to Ireland, hanging round the neck of some Viking adventurer. And now, incredibly, it has found its way home, thanks to you, William."

William was so pleased that he hopped on one leg, and said,

"But it's a key. What does it open? Keys open doors, don't they?"

Erik smiled. "Yes they do, but this probably opened a chest of valuables, hidden somewhere for safe keeping in troubled times. That was quite common. Well, here you are then, and thank you so much for bringing it in. It's a great find. A museum piece." He handed the key back to William.

William looked suddenly very unhappy.

"But, you said… Were you just being nice to me? Isn't it true?"

"Of course it's true."

"Then why can't it be in the museum?"

"—You mean," Erik broke in, "you want us to keep it?"

"I've never found a museum piece before. If it

350

was in a museum it would have a glass case and lights on it, wouldn't it?"

"It certainly would. And it would have a label saying 'Found in England and presented to the museum by…'" Erik hesitated.

"William Parkinson."

"William Parkinson, exactly."

"Would it have my name on, really?"

"I make you a solemn promise."

William was quiet for a moment, running his fingers over the faint markings on the shaft. Then he said,

"Is it all right if I keep it for a bit? I want to show Farmor the runes. But then can I have it in the museum?"

"It is yours to do with as you please. If you allow us to take care of it, then on behalf of the municipal museum and the Swedish department of Antiquities, I thank you for your generous donation."

When they left the museum William was possibly the happiest person in Sweden.

*

Judy was a bit different when she returned from her talk to Rashid: quiet, but not closed off at all. When Stefan asked her how it had gone she said,

"It was all right in the end. He understands, I think. We're going to keep in touch, and Soheila is a good person." That was all there was time for on the bus journey home, because William had to tell Judy about his find, which took quite a long time, and then he had to know when she thought the glass case would be ready, and the label with his name on it.

As soon as they got home William rushed in to the kitchen to show Farmor the runes and tell her all about their visit. In the hall, taking off her boots, Judy saw her windcheater hanging from a peg and remembered something. She fished the object that she had picked up on her day out with Stefan out of the pocket. She called out,

"William, I've got something for you." He was delighted, looking at it very intently from every side, saying thank you a lot of times, asking questions and wondering if she was sure that it really was for him. She was sure.

William shook it.

"There's something inside it."

"Let's go to the workshop and get it open," said Stefan, who had emerged from the kitchen with an empty woodbasket.

"No. Here's the keyhole," declared William. There was indeed an oblong hole, still full of dirt, in one side just below the lid. "And I've got the key!"

They then spent quite a lot of time explaining to William that a key could not just open any box; it had to be the right box. William got upset, positively shirty, and said that he knew that perfectly well, but he just knew that he would find the box after talking to the men at the museum and now he had found it, or rather they had found it.

"But, William, you must see that the chances of finding the right box are just … non-existent," said Judy despairingly.

But William would not be moved. So of course, they had to try it.

In the kitchen Farmor took the box to the sink and rinsed out the small oblong hole as well as she could. As she did so, she saw marks just below the hole.

"Oh look," she said, "there are runes here too!" Then she placed the box ceremoniously on the kitchen table, and they all gathered round.

William took the forked end of his key and poked it into the hole. It went in quite easily.

But that means nothing, thought Judy, *it's not exactly a sophisticated piece of engineering*. William jiggled the key about a bit, but nothing happened.

Judy had been thinking. The lock must be simple enough, you could tell that by the key, so how could a simple three-dimensional key engage with a relatively straightforward fastening mechanism?

"Can I have a go?" She asked William. He handed over the key, with a disappointed look.

"It's no good – it isn't the right key."

Judy inserted the key. She didn't expect anything to happen, but she tried the various possible combinations of movements. On the third try, she pressed the key up a little, felt it catch on something, and pushed. A small gap opened between the lid and the box.

"It worked – it *is* the right key!" William was beside himself.

Farmor gasped. Stefan shook his head in amazement and thumped William on the back.

"The man said that the key had come home," gabbled William, "and it has come home to its box. And the box was under a tree, just like the key, wasn't it? And it was the same storm, wasn't it? And Mr Balderson said that there were patterns and fate and … and…"

Judy knew exactly how Mr Balderson would have reacted. It was almost as though he was standing next to them now. She could imagine him nodding his head cheerfully and expanding at length on life's amazing tapestry, the warp and weft of fate, and a great deal more besides.

Stefan couldn't stand it any more.

"Open it, William, for the sake of goodness, open it."

William opened it, and they all peered inside.

They saw only some dry brown debris, like the sweepings from an outhouse or the woodshed. Stefan pushed his fingers into it, and pulled out a thin, leaf-like wafer, hardly as long as his thumb. It glinted in the light from the kitchen lamp, and there was never a moment's doubt. It was gold. Only gold emerges after a thousand-year rest as bright and untarnished as the day it was hidden. Stefan laid it carefully on the table, and four heads bent over it, and studied the figure embossed on the surface. William was the first to speak.

"It's Mr Balderson! How did he get there?"

The figure of a man that they were gazing at was simply worked, almost primitive, with long hair, a determined look, and only one eye. There was no doubt who it brought to mind.

23

Three days later, after deciding that rather than stand any more of William's nagging they would take the bus to Timbuktu, never mind the local town, they were standing outside the door of the museum office and knocking politely. Farmor had come along too; it was just too exciting to miss. Erik the archaeologist smiled pleasantly when he saw them, and said,

"William Parkinson, nice to see you. Your label is not quite ready yet, but I promise…"

"We've found the box. The box that the key opens."

A sympathetic look came over Erik's face.

"Er, William. I know it was very exciting to make a proper museum find, but it's the sort of thing that happens once in a lifetime. Sometimes it never happens. It hasn't happened to me, and I've been on digs every summer for ten years. You should be very satisfied."

The point of this was lost on William.

"I am very satisfied. We've found the box, of course I'm satisfied."

Erik sighed. "Well, let's see it then."

William reached into the carrier bag he was carrying and put the box proudly on the desk. It didn't look like much, just an old square box, but Erik went very quiet. Then he said brusquely,

"Provenance?"

Stefan was prepared this time.

"South side, thirty metres below the summit, I've marked the exact spot with a stick." There was a large-scale map of the entire municipality on the wall, and he pointed out the place to him.

Erik picked up the box, took out his magnifying glass, and studied it. Then he put it down gently.

"Well, William, there seems to be something about you. Obviously it would be beyond ridiculous if your key opened this box, but there is no doubt…" He stopped, for he had seen the runes engraved below the keyhole. He studied them for a moment.

"Well, that is a surprise."

"What do they say?" It was Farmor who asked eagerly.

"I think, no I'm sure of it, they say *'Baldr mun koma'* – 'Balder comes again'. It's the rest of the line that was on the key – 'All ills grow better, Balder comes again'. But the key, is it possible?" Now it was Judy's turn to step forward, and ceremoniously insert the key and open the box.

Erik the archaeologist looked inside and his sharply indrawn breath told his visitors all they needed to know. Then he got up, went to the door which led to an inner room, and called,

"Henrik, come here please, immediately."

The older bearded archaeologist entered, and Erik gestured to the box. When he had looked inside for a long moment he raised his eyes to the expectant visitors and said,

"I don't know what to say. And the box, with its key! I can't believe this isn't some kind of hoax."

"It certainly is not a hoax," said Farmor. "What an idea, indeed."

"No, no, but it is too much to take in all at once. He addressed William. "As one archaeologist to another, I must ask you for a favour."

"What?" said William. He was immune to flattery. He didn't even know it was happening most of the time.

"Leave this box here for a day or two – a week at the most. Then Erik will personally return it to you, together with the key, and you must make your own decisions about what to do with them."

It took some persuading from the others to get William to agree. He thought a week was a very long time. But they had seen the look on Erik's face.

It was the longest week in William's life by far. Stefan was at school a lot, and Matilda was approaching her time, so Judy had to keep an eye on her. Farmor took the brunt of it, as usual, telling William all the local tales and legends, particularly those to do with the hill beyond the marsh, where strange sights were seen at midsummer, and on New Year's night, and strange plants grew that grew nowhere else.

But at last one afternoon a car drove up the track, now rutted and muddy as the thaw set in properly, and Erik stepped out, carrying a holdall. He was greeted kindly by Farmor and offered coffee, but it was no good imagining he would be able to drink it and chat for a while, William saw to that.

Judy and Stefan were fetched, from the stables and workshop, and sat in a row on the settle, while Erik laid the box and the key on the table.

"Now," said Erik, solemnly opening the box and withdrawing the small gold wafer, "this is definitely the strangest series of events that I or any of my colleagues have ever encountered. If I was not a confirmed rationalist, I would be talking of magic or miracles. This little golden image," he went on "is known as a *guldgubbe* – I think there is no proper English word for it, it means simply gold old man. And it is clearly a representation of Odin. In itself these objects are not unfamiliar to archaeologists;two or three thousand of them have come to light. They were made as small offerings to the gods and placed in the sacred shrines to Odin,

Thor, and the other deities of the Norse religion. But none has ever been found much North of Uppsala, and indeed there has until recently been very little known about how or where the old gods were worshipped. There is of course a very full description of the temple in Uppsala by Adam of Bremen, but a lot of doubt has been cast on his words, on account of his Christian bias, and since most of the building was in wood, and the early Christianisers of Scandinavia made sure to erect their churches on the old sacred sites, we are surprisingly ignorant…" Erik stopped himself. He could see that his audience was beginning to be a bit impatient. "However, what is of course interesting here is the enormous amount of questions that need answering. Somebody deposits a sacred image on a hill here, but locked in a box, and then apparently goes off on his travels with the key in his pocket. Was he afraid of it being taken from the shrine where it lay? That is likely, if he held firmly to the old beliefs in the face of encroaching Christianity, and did not know what he would find when he returned. And whatever the answer to that question, he cannot have deposited it just anywhere. The place where he hid it must have been special. Was it a place sacred to the old gods, far to the North where the Christian missionaries had as yet made no progress – indeed, had met serious opposition?"

"A missionary was hacked to pieces by the followers of Thor near here," said Farmor. "Everyone knows that."

"It was under something, the box, it could have been an old wooden floor or something," Stefan added.

"As I suspected. The place must have had special significance – a rock formation, a sacred grove, a source of water, for example."

"The spring is there, the one that never freezes," said Judy.

"We call it Walter's well," said Farmor, "but nobody remembers who he was."

"That just about clinches it, I would say. Almost certainly a corruption of 'Valtyr's', one of the many names of Odin. It means the slain god. And that connects perfectly with the runes on the box and the key, which of course refer to the twilight of the gods, Ragnarok, when Odin dies, and to the return of life to middle earth, when his son Balder walks again. And to the followers of Odin, every well or spring would represent the well of Mimir, where Odin's eye lies hidden."

There was a lot to take in. William said,

"It is a proper museum find, isn't it?" Erik laughed happily.

"That hardly covers it, William. There are about ten full-scale PhDs to be had from this find, and one of them is going to be mine, I can tell you that. But first, of course, we have to do several hard summers up on the hill where you found this. There might well have been a temple there, the first ever found in the north. There may be indications of connections to Norway, or to the Viking settlements further afield. And that ash tree! Is it the scion of a scion of some sacred tree over there in the North of England? We shall see."

William positively glowed.

"But now I must ask you, Mrs Petterson," Erik went on, "whether there will be any objection to full-scale investigation starting already this summer.

I gather that it is your land."

"Well, certainly no objection from me, but there might be from Scandinavian Wood."

"What have they got to do with it?"

"We are selling. They will move in and start clear-felling as soon as the marsh holds next winter."

"No! It is impossible! Have you signed your contract?"

"Not yet, but we don't have much choice, I'm afraid."

"Oh yes you do. This is a national interest – international. There will be a positive pilgrimage up here. It will be worth millions to the municipality, jobs, everything. And the National Archaeological Institute has funds set aside for just this kind of thing. Sign nothing! Promise me. You will not lose by it, I can assure you." Farmor looked dazed.

Then Erik turned to William.

"William, I must now tell you that in view of the importance of these objects, I could find some way of twisting your arm…" William looked worried, because he didn't want his arm twisted "However, I do not want to do that. So I shall ask you, beg you, to consider leaving them voluntarily in our care. There will not be a glass case…" He smiled at William's frown, and went on. "There will be a William Parkinson Room in the new museum wing, displaying the finds, and a proper wallchart with information about how they came to light thanks to you and your determined interest."

"That would be very nice, but it must say that Judy and Stefan found the box."

"Of course. Everything will be true and right."

24

Judy was in the loose box talking to Matilda, who was less interested in her than she used to be. Most of Matilda's attention was focused on the wobbly, ridiculously long-legged thing that was butting at her underneath, trying to find somewhere to suckle. Judy was tired and dishevelled. She had been up most of the night to help out, though it had turned out not to be necessary really. Matilda had managed quite well on her own. Now Judy said,

"So you're all right too, aren't you? There's some stuff left to sort out, like what on earth we're going to tell the police when William finally shows up at home, but basically it's end of story. As for me..." She wiped off her hands, picked some straw out of her hair, and went out to join the others. They sat on a low plank bench with their backs to the timbered gable of the barn, the sun full in their faces, warm at last.

Stefan was in his shirtsleeves, Farmor bareheaded, her wrinkled features at peace. She was not planning her funeral, as she was just a short time ago, but planning her vegetable garden. Runner beans this year, and something new perhaps, that she hasn't tried before – there are always new varieties turning up, especially in the world of beans and brassicas.

Judy sat down beside her. She was not planning anything, but she was among friends. Farmor left her vegetables for a moment and thought about the girl who was now leaning her head against her shoulder. She would live on, grow up, do something different and decent. She would carry the indelible marks, tattooed on her soul, and it would set her apart. People would recognize her as fearless; she had always been that, but now she would do what had to be done with no heed to the consequences to herself, unattached. Bad people will not love her.

Good people will follow her.

The sound of a rattling, wheezing engine broke in on Farmor's thoughts. Stefan sat up. A diesel, but in a terrible state – a lot of gear changes as it struggled up the track. Aristeas the camper limped up the hill. He was not well. Stefan heard the uneven piston strokes – three cylinders at the most. The engine was done for, the suspension wrecked, the whole vehicle listed horribly. Clutch and gearbox not much better, Stefan guessed, the windscreen cracked right across; and as the camper rolled agonizingly into the farmyard, he saw a horizontal gash right along its side, as though it had met a snowplough coming the other way on a narrow road. Stefan knew that this time it would be the scrapyard.

They all stood up, except for Judy. She watched the camper coming into the yard. Here he comes again. Mr Balderson, the oddest person she had ever met. She had never understood him, and never would. What was he planning now? Stefan walked forward as the cab door opened. The sun was in Judy's eyes, but she saw a tall figure clambering out and heard a voice, speaking very correct English, not loud but very clear on the still air.

"Excuse me, but I was told that a Stefan Petterson lived here."

"I am Stef…"

Stefan didn't get any further, for the man had been suddenly assaulted by a tornado of arms and flying dark hair, a tornado that now wept and sobbed and seemed to want to strangle him. There were no words for quite a long time, and when at last they came they were gently murmured Persian words, answered only by gulps and sniffs, while a hand stroked the dark head. They were spoken by a man with well-cut features, dark eyebrows and a beaky nose.

Nobody else spoke. The man fell silent, but he didn't try to move. He seemed to think it would be perfectly all right to be hugged to death.

And then high above them, an abandoned, free, heart-stopping cry that echoed and echoed and echoed across the still valley, and was answered by another, and another. There is no sound like it in the world. There cannot be.

"Oh God bless us all," said Farmor, "the cranes have come."

Every face, even Judy's, turned upwards, and they saw two great long-necked, long-legged birds glide on wide wings low over the farm, crying their wild greeting. "We have come back. We always come back. It is spring."

And they sailed on, to settle on the marsh.

25

It took a very long time, in William's view, before he could get answers to some of the more important questions. There were the ones that everybody wanted the answers to, such as why Rashid had said Mr Azad was dead when he wasn't, and where Mr Balderson had gone, and also some of his own, such as whether Judy's father really was the only other person in the world who never cheated and never lied, as Judy had said, and also, if they were going into the town to talk to Rashid, whether he could come with them and see how they were getting along with the William Parkinson Room. He had started to ask almost immediately, when Judy had got herself a bit untangled from him, but Stefan had said, "End of conversation," in a very determined voice, and he and Farmor had taken him inside, while Judy and her father sat on the bench.

But in the end they came in, and Judy introduced everybody, and Farmor sat them all down at the kitchen table and produced buns and biscuits and coffee.

Judy's father was pale, and hadn't shaved for quite a long time, but William could see in his eyes, which were dark brown just like Judy's, that he was very happy, especially when he looked at Judy. She had been crying quite a lot, and her face was puffy, but she was happy too.

Mr Azad took a cup of coffee from Farmor's hands and sipped it.

"Ah, coffee. Real, honest, strong coffee. Now everything really is perfect." And he thanked Farmor, and Stefan and William for looking after his daughter and giving her so much, although William was quick to point out that he hadn't given Judy anything, it was she who had given him the box, and then Judy said, "William, you have given me lots and lots," but when he wanted to ask her what things, then it had to be end of conversation again. But she did say that she would explain later. Then Mr Azad started to talk.

"Poor Rashid," he said. "My poor dear friend, how could he know? "

Stefan had to concentrate quite hard as Mr Azad unfolded his tale, because although he spoke very clearly he was the kind of person who didn't use a short word if a long one would do. But in the end, with Judy and William asking questions, and Farmor explaining sometimes in rapid Swedish asides, he got the story straight.

When Mr Azad discovered to his dismay that he had allowed himself to be fooled by the letter, he was at a loss.

"Rashid never even arrived in Sweden! That nice woman at the asylum centre who had posted it, Soheila…" Now William broke in and said that she wasn't at the asylum centre, she was a cleaning lady at the museum, and she had told him about the key. After a bit of explaining, and several people round the table saying that they could talk lots about the key later, Mr Azad went on. He had talked for a long time to Soheila, about where she had met Rashid, and where he was heading, so he at least had some idea of what to do.

"I had a pretty good idea of what he would try. We had talked so many times of the best routes when we were younger. We even went on little expeditions, you understand, to *reconnoitre*."

'*Reconnoitre*' was a word that flummoxed both Stefan and William. When it was sorted out he said, "So off I went, Judy." He looked at his daughter. "If I had known…"

His search took him further and further back along the refugee trail, and in the end there was nothing for it, he had to cross the border.

"I had very convincing papers. They cost me a lot of money."

Once there, said Mr Azad, he soon found out that Rashid had been taken quite early on his flight, brought back and imprisoned. By bribing the right people, and "calling in some old favours" as he put it, he had managed to organize Rashid's escape, and they had fled in a friend's car. But it went wrong, and they knew they were being hunted. They had to abandon their car and make way on foot. In the end they became separated. Mr Azad had been caught and had prepared himself to die. But then came the surprise. His captors knew perfectly well who he was and wanted him alive. They weren't particularly interested in Rashid.

"How did they know it was you?" William had to ask. Mr Azad looked at him and sighed.

"Well, someone must have told them, don't you think?"

"Someone who knew who you were?"

"Yes. I am fairly sure who it was. An old friend. Someone I trusted."

"But he wasn't your friend any more."

Mr Azad was silent for a moment. Then he said,

"I suppose not. But betrayal is seldom cut and dried. Life asks a lot of us, sometimes too much."

Farmor had been listening quietly.

"It does, Mr Azad. It does."

"But I will say this. True friendship, if it ever comes your way, is a pearl without price." Now he looked again at Judy. They had a lot of talking to do, but there was time.

Mr Azad returned to his story.

His captors fired their guns into the air, took off his jacket and fired into it, riddling it with bullet holes, took his papers and few possessions, smeared them with blood ("they cut my arm to get it, but under the circumstances I wasn't complaining") and scattered them across a hillside. Then they bundled him into a car. It was his expertise they needed. Lots of engineers and computer experts and mathematicians had fled the country, and they needed him. They knew all about the work he had been doing; that he was a physicist and engineer.

"Well," said Mr Azad, "they succeeded very well in convincing poor Rashid that I was dead. They even put out one of those horrible announcements saying that the traitor Azad had been brought to justice and disposed of. So I didn't exist."

"They were lying," William remarked.

"They were indeed. That is their hallmark, their speciality."

After that followed a hard time. He didn't want

to talk about it much. He had no intention of doing the kind of secret work that they wanted; it had to do with weapons – nuclear weapons, he soon realized. But they told him that he would never see his daughter again if he didn't, that they knew where she was, that they had full surveillance. He knew they were lying about that, he trusted her, but he pretended to give in. There was no other hope of seeing Judy again. So now he was treated like royalty.

"Didn't they lock you up? Kings aren't locked up."

"Well, perhaps they are not locked up, exactly. But kings have bodyguards watching them all the time, and they can't ever go out by themselves. And they get nice food."

But Mr Azad was only waiting for the right moment. He had decided from the first that he would get back to Judy somehow. He knew he might die if he tried, and thought about that for a long time – he had lain awake one whole night. He had decided that it would be better for her to have a dead father than a father in a faraway country making bombs.

In the end his chance came. He was being driven to a research facility in the desert, and when the car broke down and the driver and his bodyguard had their heads under the bonnet, he simply threw himself out of the car and ran.

"No careful planning. I just ran."

He ran, and then he walked, and walked and walked.

"At the end, to be honest with you, I crawled. But I came to the only place I knew where I could find help." It was the village where he had been born. "And where you too, Judy, first saw the light of day. You don't remember that village – but it remembers you. I was given water, a place to lay my head. I slept for two days. When I woke it was time to plan the next part of my journey. With no papers and no money, how was I to leave the country? I went to the little café, to think things over, and there, sitting at a table in the shade and drinking peppermint tea, was my deus ex machina, Andrew Balderson."

A babble of voices erupted round the table. Even Farmor had something to say. William got nowhere with his question about what a deus ex machina was. Mr Azad calmly sipped his coffee, smiling in satisfaction at the dramatic effect he had created.

"But … you *know* him?" Judy asked, when things had quietened down a bit. "You can't."

"Why can't I? We have met in the public library on several occasions and had some very interesting conversations – a fine scholar and a great traveller. He was very well up on the Sufis, we—"

Suddenly a thought struck Judy. "The second valley, he said you would know."

"Of course. Attar. Mantiq Ut-Tair. The Conference of the Birds, they call it in English. The seven valleys."

"But the *second* valley?"

"The second valley, Judy, is the valley of love and true friendship. A hard valley to cross. Andrew is a learned man, but even so I was able to put him in the way of some of the minor poets. And he had never read Zeb-Un-Nissa: a shocking omission, as I said to him at the time. A wonderful poet, and one of the few women who…"

"Dad."

"Of course. Where was I?"

Mr Balderson had offered him a lift home, and he had been glad to accept.

"So I crossed the border squashed into one of his storage lockers, under the couch."

"Just like me!" William was delighted. "I did too!"

The journey had been long, and full of difficulties. They had gone north, and managed to reach the Russian border, and then on towards Finland. Then one day they came to a beautiful lake, with an island in the middle. On the island was an old monastery, it was called:

"Valamo," said Farmor.

"Indeed, Mrs Petterson, Valamo. A more serene and spiritual place I have never seen. We rested for a while, being very kindly looked after, and when the time came to go on (I was rather impatient to find you, as you can imagine, Judy) Andrew said no.

"'I have stopped now, Reza, and I shall not start again. I have seen enough, and done enough, and read enough. I'm full to bursting, and it is time to start emptying stuff out.'

"That's what he said. And he led me to a little hermitage in the woods behind the monastery, that he had been told he could occupy. Remarkable people, the monks of Valamo. He showed me where he would sleep, I was astounded, it was…"

"A coffin," said Judy.

"Yes, how did you know? He would sleep in a coffin!"

And that was it. Mr Azad set off alone, and here he was.

Farmor sighed contentedly. She wasn't the slightest bit surprised that Mr Balderson had turned up when he was needed. But Stefan was stunned.

"But how could he find … there are so many places; the world is a very big place I think?"

Judy had been thinking hard.

"I think I know. We met some people at a campsite. And I told him the name of the village that Dad… That we come from."

"Ha!" said Mr Azad, "It still works, I find," and he

tapped Judy gently on the head with his forefinger. "Indeed, Judy. I asked Andrew the very same question, and he said to me, "Reza, where does a man go when there is nowhere else to go? Who takes a man in, when all refuse him succour? He goes home, Reza, he goes home. Just as a fugue returns to its home key, a man wends his way through the music of his life... Oh well, you know how he talks."

Yes, they said laughing, they did know. There was quite a lot of laughing after that, and talking and eating cinnamon buns and discussing Norse mythology, which Reza Azad showed a lot of interest in, to William's great satisfaction. At one point Judy, who was sitting very close to her father, asked quietly,

"Did you tell anybody else that you were going away? Or was it only me?"

"Well," came the soft reply, "I might possibly have mentioned it to Andrew Balderson..."

And what about poor Rashid? Farmor apologized to Mr Azad for shooting his best friend and was instantly forgiven. She rang Soheila's apartment, and prepared her a bit, and then Reza spoke to Rashid. Nobody understood what he said, apart from Judy, and that was probably for the best.

26

The next day was beautiful. The spring sun warmed the farm and started mopping up the last of the snow. Even on the north side of the house there was only a dwindling heap left. Farmor found the first coltsfoot by the meadow fence. Then Rashid and Soheila arrived in Rashid's little car, and soon after that the man from the scrapyard came driving an old rescue vehicle with a winch, and he and Stefan spent some time manoeuvring Aristeas on to it for his final journey. So before she knew it, Farmor had a party on her hands. She rushed off to the kitchen and Judy ran to help her.

"Cupcakes," said Farmor. "Are they hard to make?"

"Not too hard," said Judy, "if you know how."

They laid tables out of doors for the very first time that year, and there was coffee and blackcurrant juice and bread and cheese, there were pancakes with whipped cream and cloudberry jam and then, triumphantly, Judy appeared with a tray of newly iced cupcakes. Her father was so moved that he stood up and made a speech to the honour of the noble cupcake and all it meant for human civilization. Then the man from the scrapyard, who had only sat with them on Farmor's insistence, because he was wearing greasy overalls over a dirty T-shirt, and a cap with "John Deere" on the peak, got up and went to his truck, coming back with a suitcase of some kind. He opened it and took out an accordion. Then he said something to Stefan. Stefan went into the house and came out with a violin. He stuck it under his chin, and they started to play. It was strange music, some of it fast and dancing, some of it slow and winding, in minor keys with odd harmonies. It was music for forests, and mountains, and lakes and rivers and hard work.

Judy sat beside Farmor.

"I didn't know that Stefan…"

"Oh, here everybody plays. Well, not everybody. But Stefan is fifth generation. His great-great-grandfather made the one they are playing now. He is born to it."

When they stopped, to eat some more and drink more coffee, Judy said,

"You never told me you played the violin, Stefan."

Stefan looked at her and grinned.

"So? It is not good for you to know everything."

THE END

THE END

ABOUT THE AUTHOR

Toby Ibbotson grew up in Newcastle upon Tyne. After university, he planned to travel the world – and he made it as far as Sweden, where he has lived ever since. His home is in the north of the country, where winters are long, dark and cold but spring is a real spring. Toby has a wonderful wife and two beloved children as well as two small dogs, nine bean rows and a honeybee hive. He has been a teacher for over thirty years.